JORDYN MERYL

THE LIGHTNING CREST

The Lightning Crest
by
Jordyn Meryl

Published by jm dragonfly, L.L.C.
Des Moines, IA

ISBN-13:978-1511924375
ISBN-10:1511924373

Printed in the United States of America

Other Books
By
Jordyn Meryl

Italian Dream Series
When Dream Change-Book 1
When Dream Collide-Book 2
When Dream Die-Books 3

The Trouble With Angels
Home Before Dark
The Space Between-A Paranormal Romantic Suspense

Coming Soon
Katie's Wind
The House of the Crescent Moon

DEDICATION

Not a day goes by that I am not grateful for the blessings I have received. I am truly blessed with family and friends that support and love me. Life is good.

The writer's group at Smokey Row have become a precious asset to my writing and my life. Thank you Sue, Lavina, Julie, Larry and Matt.

This story was a stretch for me, but my beta readers Sue, Lorene, Jen, Jan and Tina said to "go for it". So I am.

To Nick Miller, strategy adviser "On How to Catch a Traitor."

This story planted its seed long ago. It was lost for a while, but kept nagging at me to write it so it could be set free. Here it is, in all its glory. Once again I have been guided by a loving God, a gracious Universe and Karma, the seeker of justice.

Please support me by:

Leaving a review at-

Amazon

Goodreads

My Facebook page

Telling your friends and family

An author is judged

by the feedback Of their readers.

Thank you,

jm

CHAPTER ONE

Listen, you will hear it

A commanding voice circled around the lone rider on horseback. Bowing her head, Rayn listened for the promised sounds. The faint sound of marching feet, the creak of leather being mounted told her what she waited to know. Raising her head to the west, she shaded her eyes against the sun with her hand. The warm summer wind whipped around her lookout point, a bluff high above the Fort. She shifted slightly in the saddle. Hearing the low hum of motorcycles radiating up, she immediately determined the direction they were headed. Turning her horse to the south, her heels dug into his sides, giving him full reins. Galloping ahead of the noise of the troops, the horse flew down the hills, over the fields to a lone farmhouse hidden behind a row of tall poplar trees.

When Rayn reached the front of the house, she slid off the horse, throwing the reins to the man waiting for her return. Bounding up the steps two at a time, her boots hitting the wooden steps, she burst into the house.

"Get the children below!" Her voice thundered with the command.

The adults moved swiftly, grabbing up the children, steering them toward a wall that opened to reveal steps going down into a tunnel. Down the steps, the children moved rapidly, without a sound. Running silently, they followed the adults through the darkness. When they reached a large open room, each took their place on the benches.

Without a sound, they sat holding hands with their heads bent in quiet prayer. As the last adult entered the room, they looked up with fear in their eyes. The adults move to sit next to the younger children, hugging them, speaking with soft, reassuring, trusting voices.

On the main floor, Rayn turned to her-son-law standing next to her.

"Archer, we have about ten minutes. They're coming this way." Her tone portrayed the urgency of the moment. "Hit the alarm."

Archer nodded, pressing a device on his wrist, then moved swiftly to the outside. Using only hand signals, he motioned to the men standing below the deck to take their places. The wall of books hiding the entrance to the cellar moved smoothly back into position, leaving no trace. Rayn walked promptly outside, ambled gracefully and calmly down the steps, her back straight. As she reached the ground, a squadron of motorcyclists entered the yard. Led by a young lieutenant, the riders were dressed in black with yellow stripes to indicate they were of the Cartel.

Standing with her hands on her hips, Rayn kept her eyes on the lead rider. He stopped, his eyes covered with dark glasses; she could still feel his stare on her. Settling the cycle, he swung his leg off, standing tall and straight on the ground. As she watched him, she thought he moved with the ease of a jungle cat stalking his prey. Her eyes travel down his masculine youthful form. A smile played at the corner of her mouth as she admired the tight, fit, body of a soldier. He took off his hat, removed his glasses. His smile insincere as he walked toward her.

"Rayn. It is good to see you again" His electric blue-gray eyes sparkled in a handsome face.

"Lieutenant Konner. What gives us the pleasure of your company?" She could feel the tension that hummed between them.

"Checking for children." He held her gaze.

"Do I look like I have children?" Her long dark hair fell against her shoulders as she faced him, arms crossed.

"Not yours personally. Just any children in general" His gaze moved down her curvy frame in a white t-shirt under a denim blue shirt and faded jeans. She shifted uncomfortably under his stare

"Look around." Rayn waved her arms in the air.

Lieutenant Konner jerked his head toward the men behind him. Half of them dismounted, spread out, some around the yard, some to the house, and some to the barn. The other half drove over the fields and the pastures, to check the out-buildings.

Archer stood against the fence, watching with a stony look. A pretty, young girl came silently to his side, encircling his waist, leaned against him.

With her back rigid, Rayn walked over to the deck steps, turned around to face the Lieutenant. Keeping her eyes on him, she sat down. Lieutenant Konner smiled, cutting the distance between them with long, purposeful strides. He placed one foot on the step next to her, leaned down. He ran his finger along her hairline, picking up the moisture from her face.

"You're sweating, Rayn." His touch was a feather-light caress, his look dark and dangerous.

"It's a hot day." She moved her head from his sensual touch, grabbing the railing to pull herself up. He stopped her with his hand on her arm.

"Rayn, make this easy on yourself. Give me the children and I'll get you out of this mess."

She clenched her fists. "I told you, there are no children here! And what makes you think I'm in a mess?"

He leaned closer. "You don't want to find out what they can do to you. You will not win this!" He turned his head, his voice low, masculine and oh so sure of himself. "I can make sure you are safe."

Rayn stood abruptly, drawing her hand back ready to smack the cocky son-of-a-bitch. The Lieutenant grabbed it, pinned it behind her, bringing her into his body. He smiled slow, daring at her.

Out of the corner of her eye, she saw Archer detached himself from the fence, moving quickly to her side. She put out her free arm to stop his attack on the lieutenant.

"Yes Rayn, hold your son-in law back. " Lieutenant Konner's voice flat, calm full of taunting.

Archer lunged, but Rayn held him. "No! Archer! Stop!" She looked at the lieutenant with disgust. "Leave him alone!"

Konner stepped back, released her. "I will, as soon as you give me the children." Anger narrowed his eyes, stiffening his jaw.

"I told you, there are no children." She felt her temper rise, but worked to keep it in check.

The soldiers came out of the house, stood at the top of the deck. "There are no children." The tall one said.

Rayn cocked her head at the lieutenant, gave him a smug smile. Lieutenant Konner glared at her. His eyes betrayed his frustration at not being able to prove she was lying.

"Mount up!" He shouted to his men. They ran to their cycles, jumping onto the seats, straddled the machines, legs stiff, ready to go. As the men waited, he spit out his words. "Next time, and there will be a next time, I will find them!" His voice was low and laced with anger.

"Be my guest." His doubting expression was really beginning to piss her off.

Walking past her, he swung easily onto his cycle. With one last look he turned, with his men following, they left the yard.

"Rayn..." Archer started to apologize.

Looking into the eyes of her dear son-in-law, she reached up and cupped his cheek in her hand. "It's ok, Archer. No harm done."

The young girl came up to his side. "Mom?"

Rayn gave her daughter a smile. "Luna. We're okay for now. He's bluffing."

The men and women who had hidden during the raid were now gathering around them. She turned to them with a confident smile.

"Get the children." Her voice full of the compassion she felt deep inside.

4

***

Morning broke into brilliant colors as dawn streaked across the sky. Rayn worked in her mind, going over about how life had changed in such a short time. Once there were families, parents and children. Now no families were allowed. Children belonged to the New Cartel. Feeling that the cause of the economic downfall of the world was the children's fault, the government now took the children to raise "properly".

Archer came up behind her, interrupting her thoughts. "Hey Rayn..."

She jumped. He steadied her with his hand.

"...what's wrong with you?" Concern filled his voice.

"Nothing, lost in thought. Good morning." She hugged him.

After getting a cup of coffee, he leaned against the counter. "So, anything new today?"

"Not yet." Sighing deeply, she walked over to a big dining table, sat down. He followed, sitting across from her. Taking her hand, he tried to sound convincing.

"We'll know if they are coming. Word will get to us." The young man shook his head. "How did we get to this point?"

Smiling with pride, she lifted his chin with one finger. "We got here, because we could not watch as the children were removed from parents who loved them. We got here..." Her voice took a sorrowful edge. "...because you and Luna will have children one day and do not want them taken away."

Rayn knew Archer understood the importance of their mission. Fearful all the time, he never relaxed his guard. Together they would find a way to protect the children. They believed parents should, could raise good children. He wanted to be a father someday, did not want his children ripped from his arms. It was a dangerous place to be, but they had no other choice. Their belief in the abilities of the human race to survive itself drove them onward.

The cell phone on the counter rang. Looking at each other, Rayn moved quickly to answer it. Archer watched her listen to the person on the phone, her eyes formed tears. Moving instantly to her side, he held her steady as she hung up. Taking a deep breath, her fear closed like a fist around her heart. "The fighting starts tonight."

After breakfast, Rayn briefed the adults on what she knew. Standing before them at the table, she exuded a powerful presence. Talking with confidence, she told it to them straight. "There is a raid planned on one of the safe houses tonight. It doesn't sound like it is us, but we don't know that for sure. There's guns and ammunition behind the door. Use them only in an emergency. Keep the children downstairs until we know for sure what is happening."

The women did not cry. Rayn had all the faith in the world in them. They knew what was expected, knew what they were protecting. Like animals, they would do whatever it took to stop whatever came at them. Through struggle and determination, they had become strong.

Rayn admired the men putting aside egos to allow her to lead them. Had they not trusted her, they would have lost their families. Some of the adults were married, had made the decision together. Some had come alone in the night, fleeing the New Cartel and a partner who could not agree with the choice. However they came, they stood firm in their belief and commitment once here. Each had a duty, a post, a key part in the mission. They lived, slept and breathed the Cause.

The children were already in the underground room. Occupying them with schoolwork and games, Rayn told the adults to never hide the truth from them. If asked, they were to be told the truth, as children only fear the unknown. If need be, children would rise to the level of their expectations. These children were expected to understand that the way of life they had was not a choice, but a necessity. Adjusting with guidance and love, they thrived.

"Rayn..." Seth yelled across the house.

Feeling a burning lump form in her stomach, she ran to the command room. "What?" She was breathless, standing behind his chair.

The master communicator was Seth, a young scholar intellect with a wife and two baby girls. A techno geek of the superior kind, he built a complex, but impressive computer system. Gathering as many types of devices, some dug out of the trash plies of the Cartel, as he could get his hands on, he created a system that connected all the Insurgent bases, including penetrating the main frame in the Fort. The discarded equipment was supposedly "dumped", but crucial information could still be found deep in the hard drives. Monitoring the transmissions coming from all different sources, he directed his crew to keep track of the bouncing waves, avoiding the dark web that could destroy the Insurgent's Cause.

"Edward, catch that orphan ray." Edward nodded, producing an image on a large panel on the wall.

"The troops are moving to the northeast, toward the last house on the out skirts of town." Seth spoke as his fingers moved the images on his screen, transferring the icons to one of the big screens.

"Galen's house! How did they find them?" Rayn struggled to keep the desperation out of her voice.

"I don't know, but they are moving like they are pretty sure of their directions." Seth grimaced.

"It's coming on the Cable!" Edward pointed to another large panel on the wall.

Everyone turned to look at the big screen on the wall. The scene that unfolded before them was horrifying. Armed guards stormed the house. Kicking down the doors, they entered with guns held high, ready to fire. The cameras on their helmets showed them moving from room to room.

Rayn had her hands clasped in front of her.

Oh, God! She pleaded. *Don't let them find the children!*

Finding only empty rooms, they moved toward a spot on the floor. Surrounding the center of the room, they stood ready, guns aimed. One soldier stomped his foot and the floor opened up reveling a stairway to the cellar. As they descended the steps, Rayn felt the anticipation bring fear to her throat. After what seemed like an eternity, they reach a room. Kicking in the door, they enter cautiously, expecting to find children and adults huddled in corners. They found nothing.

"What the hell!" The first soldier shouted. Lowering his gun, he spun around to face the troop of men that followed him into the room. "Where are the children?"

The men murmured.

"What?" He shouted again, a vein near his left eye bulged as his face grew red.

The soldier standing closest to him answered shakily. "We don't know, General Bono. We were told they would be here." He looked around pleadingly at the rest of the men. They backed away from him. Standing alone, he turned to face the leader again.

"General Bono, Sir, I don't know what went wrong, sir!" He snapped to attention.

"Get out of my way, you fucking idiots." General Bono stormed pass the young soldier, the other men parted as he thundered up the stairs.

"Tear this place apart. Find the children!" He shouted his commands to anyone in his way.

Men scurried away, going to look anywhere they could. The general stomped out of the house to the officers waiting outside. Rayn took in a silent breath. One of the men was Lieutenant Konner. He made the motion to kill the sound, but the officer's actions showed his ranting and raving. The people in the command room let out a breath of relief at the same time. Suddenly, the cameras shut off, the big screen went black. Everyone turned back to look at Seth.

"They killed the cameras and sound, but I can still get the transmissions on the military bands. They are madder than hell." He smirked. "They received false information. How unfortunate!"

The room full of people laughed. Hugging each other, some left to go do other tasks. Rayn moved to the next room, going to the large glass window.

Archer came up behind her. "Close call. You okay?"

Nodding, she rubbed her temples. "We got away with it this time." She swallowed past the knot of emotion lodged in her throat. Putting her hand on his shoulders, she forced back sobs that wanted to come out. Tears were to be saved for joy, not sadness or fear.

One of the adults came over to them. "Can the children come up now?" He asked.

She regained her composure. "Yes, bring up the children."

***

Two hours later, Rayn sat at the large kitchen table, waiting. At last, she heard the familiar knock she had been expecting. The knock was soft, but the pattern unmistakable. She rose, moving silently to the door, opening it wide.

"Galen. You made it." A man in his late forties with graying hair, stepped inside. They hugged, Rayn was thankful he was here.

Behind him came a group of weary looking people, children, men and women. Rayn looked back across the kitchen, saw the people of the house coming forward to welcome the nighttime visitors. Working together, they prepared food, took the small children to a place to rest.

Archer brought Galen a fresh cup of steaming coffee. Galen nodded, wrapping both hands around the oversized mug. "Thanks. It was a long, hard trip."

Rayn waited until he took a sip. "How did you get out?"

"We got a tip, thank God. It was a narrow escape. We were barely out when they began to descend."

9

Rayn led Galen to the command room. "We watched it on the screen. Seth, can you load it?"

"Sure thing."

Galen sat down in one of the big, comfortable chairs. Rayn sat on the chair's arm. As they watched the invasion of Galen's house, Rayn was drawn to the picture of Lieutenant Konner as he stood listening to the outraged commander. With no sound, his body movements and facial expressions told the story. Looking back at the house, his handsome face worded that it was impossible there was no one there. Handsome, Rayn was surprise her mind used that word. He was the enemy. He might be attractive, charming and have an indescribable sexual aura about him, but he was the enemy. She shook off the feelings. She needed to focus on the events at hand. With Galen's escape, they were sure to come here soon. She needed to be ready, physically and mentally.

***

It was at first dawn the humming roar of cycles echoed through the valley. Rayn walked out to the deck to watch as the battalion came up to the house. Two men led. Lieutenant Konner and General Bono, one mean son of a bitch.

As the motorcade stopped in the middle of the yard, Ryan prepared herself for the interrogation.

"Ms Rayn." General Bono said with an edge in his voice.

"General." She let her contempt for him sound in her voice. She looked over at Lieutenant Konner, tilted her head. "Lieutenant?"

"Ms Rayn." She resented the way his lips formed into a disarming grin, making her feel he thought she was unable to handle him or his kind.

The general's deep-booming voice brought her head back to look at him. "Ms Rayn. We raided what we thought was a safe house last night." Nodding, she folded her arms, meeting his stare. She knew he was watching her for a reaction. Facing him down, she would never revealing anything.

The general paused, waited. When she did not answer, he raised his voice. "Did you know this?"

"No, how would I?" Her voice was steady. Out of the corner of her eye, she saw the lieutenant nod.

I hope I'm amusing him.

The general narrowed his eyes. "So you know nothing!" He spit his words at her.

"Correct, General."

"I don't believe you!"

"I'm sure you don't."

"Take her, she will talk in the Fort" He shouted his command. Lieutenant Konner jumped off his cycle, hustling up the stairs to Rayn. She backed away from him, but he grabbed her, yanked her to him.

"Stop." His low tone held an air of unequivocal authority. "Don't make this worse than it should be."

She gave him a doubtful look. "Why should I trust you?"

"Who else do you have right now?"

Over his shoulder, she saw Luna and Archer. She shook her head for them to stay back. "I'm okay."

To the lieutenant she quietly agreed to his terms. "Okay, I'll go nicely, but don't relax your guard." Her voice low, laced with vehemence.

"I wouldn't think of it." His voice cold, steady as a stone.

Taking her arm, he walked her down the stairs. He guided her to his cycle. Before she could protest, he grabbed her by her waist, hoisting her onto the back, black leather seat. Climbing on in front of her, she became aware of his body, hard and firm against hers. Slowly she slipped her arms under his, leaving a feeling of tingling lust descending down her legs. Trapped against his body, the heat from his skin scorched her.

Rayn didn't like the position she was in, but she had no other options right now. Lieutenant Konner gunned the machine, driving through the cluster of men. Each turned to follow. General Bono caught up to them.

"Well..." Bono boasted. "She's a lot less resistant than I had imagined."

Rayn bristled under his words. The lieutenant whispered back to her. "Easy. You are doing just fine."

"Glad you're pleased with my behavior." She snarled back at him.

Every movement of the motorcycle made her body move against his. Her hips flowed into his, their bodies intimately and perfectly aligned to each other. Her breasts pushed against his back. Her arms holding on to his waist, her hands clasped in front just above his manhood. Pressing on, he steered the large machine over the rough dirt road, creating a friction between their bodies as she bumped against him. His scent was warm, masculine leather bringing a sweet edge of desire to her. She fought the feelings. They were unwelcome at this time, at any time.

The Fort was about a half an hour from Rayn's farm. Riding in silence, she wondered what they had in store for her this time. It seemed every time they brought her in, it got rougher. Lieutenant Konner had been on her case for over a year. Weary from the long night and no sleep, she leaned against him relaxing, for a few minutes. The rhythm of the cycle, the soothing sound of his breathing made her sleepy.

The cycles pulled up to a big white building with pillars. Jumping easily off, Lieutenant Konner pulled Rayn to the ground. As her body slipped, making contact with his, she was fully aware of his eyes on her. He moved back first, taking her arm, dragging her roughly inside.

General Bono walked ahead of them. "Take her to the interrogation room." He shouted over his shoulder.

The lieutenant towed her down the hallway, pushing her into a windowless room with a table and three chairs.

"Sit." He commanded shoving her toward the table.

She plopped down in the straight back chair, resting her elbows on the table. Smoothing her hair back from her face, she checked out the room. At first, it looked like nothing but four walls, but she found the hidden cameras. Lieutenant Konner leaned against the wall, his arms crossed. She felt the probe of his eyes. Keeping her eyes down, she looked at her hands lying in her lap.

The door burst open as the Bono came charging in. Throwing a tablet on the table, he leaned down, his breath smelled of tobacco mingled with the scent of cheap scotch.

Bellowing at her, his face red with rage. "You have quite a rap sheet. Seems you have been under investigation for some time."

Rayn didn't move. She had learned long ago that she would be wasting her breath if she tried to give any explanation.

He went on. "You are suspected of hiding children and families that are not cooperating with the Cartel.

She kept her eyes down, still said nothing.

"Answer me!" His voice rumbled like distant thunder.

She raised her eyes slowly until they were looking straight into his, held her head high. "You seem to have all the answers."

He backhanded her, knocking her off the chair. She sat up, scooted away from him, pressing her back against the wall.

Lieutenant Konner stepped between them. "Beg your pardon General, but brute force is not the best way to deal with Ms Rayn."

"And pray tell what is Lieutenant?"

"Isolation. She hates being away from her people."

General Bono looked down at Rayn with loathing in his eyes. "Fine! Imprison her!"

Rayn stared at his back as he stormed out of the room. The lieutenant walked over to Rayn, extended his hand. Ignoring it, she rose on her own to her feet. Still he kept his proximity close to her, making her uncomfortable. His eyes bore into hers, as he reached out, touching the side of her face. She flinched in pain, saw his eyes soften, but perceiving it as false compassion, shoved his hand away. Pushing her way past him, she allowed the guards to shackle her hands and feet.

Shaking her hair from her face, she clenched her jaw, looked the lieutenant square in the eye. "There are no children. Look around, the Cartel has them all."

The guards jerked her away.

Lieutenant Konner watched as they drug her down the hall, the sound of the clinking chains on the hard, concrete floor was like a knife in his heart.

CHAPTER TWO

Lieutenant Draven Konner stood at the window looking out at the fires burning below, illuminating the dark night. It was well past midnight. The dwellers of the Fort burned fires to keep vigil over the streets. His thoughts confused his mind. Seeing her in chains, restricted and imprisoned, her head bowed was not how he envisioned her. He admired the strength of her convictions. But her stubbornness escaped him.

What was so important about the children?

Rayn had captivated him long ago when he first met her. A feisty, beautiful woman, he was surprised by her moral fiber. The tension between them had taken on a sexual tone. He would wake up at night with his loins burning for her. She invaded his dreams, occupied his thoughts. Right now, she was locked up just a few feet from him and all he wanted to do was go to her. Actually, he liked her being close, though she probably didn't have the same feelings about it he did. Smiling to himself, he sighed, giving in to his need to see her.

His steps echoed down the hall as he walked to her cell. When he approached the cell doors, he slowed. She was looking out a small window with bars. Her body shifted, letting him know she knew he was there, but she wasn't acknowledging his presence. He quietly unlocked the door, slipped easily up behind her. Her back stiffened, she moved slightly away from him. He turned to look at her, angling his body to block her if she should decide to retreat.

"Rayn?"

Raising her gaze to his, her eyes reflexed the doubt she had of his good intentions. "What?"

He traced her cheek with the back of his hand, touching the purple bruise glowing against her swollen cheek. She didn't draw back, but searched his face.

"Sorry about that." He wanted her to know he was trying to be straight.

"Why, you didn't hit me?"

15

He stopped his fingers at the back of her neck, cupped her head. "I wish I could have prevented it."

Her eyes narrowed with distrust. "Why would you want to stop that?"

"Because, you don't deserve to be hit."

"Who the hell are you and what have you done with Lieutenant Konner?"

He laughed as she allowed him to pull her head against his forehead. "Fair enough. I deserved that."

He wanted to gather her to him. To protect her, but then she was quite capable of protecting herself. He felt it was getting out of hand for her, though. General Bono was ready to make someone pay for disobeying him, she was the most likely target. He had to warn her.

"Rayn..." He whispered against her hair. "...he will hurt you. Stop what you're doing. Is it worth the price?"

She stepped back from him, moving farther away with every word. "Yes. I know what I am fighting for. Do you?"

"Know what you are fighting for? No."

"What about what you are fighting for?" Her voice held a challenge.

He held his head up but he had no answer. He had never been asked what he was fighting for. She clucked her tongue to her cheek, waiting for his answer.

"Well, yeah. I guess. Of course I do. I'm a Lieutenant in the Cartel's army and I am not fighting for anything. You're the one fighting. I'm just obeying.

"Well, you sweet obeying little thing you..." Her voice dripped with a sarcastic sweetness. "...make sure you can always be obedient. For if you aren't, they will hunt you, like they hunt me."

"You could change that, Rayn!" He spoke sternly, determined she would understand the risks.

"So could you." Her voice soft but firm.

Rayn walked over to sit down on the cot. The tenacious woman gave him a look he could not read or know how to respond to. He didn't want to leave her, but she dismissed him. Starting to turn away, he turned back, wanting to speak to her. She wasn't looking at him, so he decided it was best to leave. At least she was safe tonight. He would sleep in his office so he could check on her through the night. Without a word, he reluctantly turned back, leaving her and the cell.

***

Draven stood at the sink in the bathroom off his office. He looked in the mirror, stopping for a second to think of his position. He was attracted to the enemy.

Rayn.

He wanted her to stop fighting the Cartel, let him into her life to stop all the nonsense. What amazed him, she brought such unfamiliar feelings to the surface. Raised in a loveless, military family, his feelings for her blindsided him. Wanting her sexually was not what surprised him. He had made use of several women for sex, never wanted any of them to stay. They took care of his needs then went their way. But he wanted more from Rayn. He wanted to have her with him all the time. Unable to stand being away from her, he raided her farm more than was necessary. Her words to him, about what he was fighting for, sent doubts to his mind.

Did one need a cause? A purpose?

He had never thought about it.

Dray knew she was hiding children. If he could only find them, she would give up her cause and he could take her away from all the fighting. Her being older than him by some years only made her more attractive. She was a strong, determined woman. And that made his blood boil for her.

A loud conversation in the hallway made him look out the door. General Bono and another officer were in deep debate. The young officer, Lieutenant Milo, joined as a cadet the same time as Draven.

Bono's voice boomed down the narrow hallway. "She needs to be made an example."

Lieutenant Milo shook his head. "If you do that we will have uproar."

"So what? It will bring all those Insurgents out in the open." Bono shrugged.

"Don't underestimate your enemy." The other officer spoke softly.

General Bono's voice roared, bouncing off the walls. "Don't tell me what to do!"

Draven walked out into the hall, fully dressed and ready for the day. "What's the problem, General Bono?"

General Bono whipped around, throwing his arms in the air. "That woman!"

Draven chuckled to himself. "Which woman would that be?"

"Your Ms Rayn."

"And what is your problem with her today?" Lieutenant Konner snickered. He wasn't taking anything General Bono said seriously.

Bono shook his finger in Draven's face. "She needs to be taught a lesson."

Draven raised an eyebrow. "And how do you plan on doing that, Sir?"

"Public execution." He said it with a proud tone in his voice.

Feeling the blood drain from his face, Lieutenant Konner searched the general's face. *Had he heard right?*

Draven forced the words out. "What?"

General Bono looked smugly at him. "Don't you think that's a good idea? The Insurgents will come unglued."

"Unglued!" Draven looked over at Milo. "They will attack us all. Where did this lame brain idea come from?"

General Bono patted his chest. "Lame brain! I'm the lame brain. I think it's a good idea. End some of this rubbish about saving the children."

Draven could not think of a thing to say.

Am I really taking commands from a man that wants to publicly execute a woman?

Finally he spoke. "Surely there is a better way."

"No, tomorrow at noon. We will get rid of the Insurgents finally. Prepare for an execution." General Bono dismissed the two officers, strolled proudly down the hall.

Draven looked at Milo. He offered no help, just lowered his head and walked away. A feeling of being trapped in a bad situation came over Draven. He didn't know what he was going to do, but he knew he could not stand by and let Rayn die. Not if there was some way to stop it.

But how?

He walked into his office, slammed the door, leaning against it. He had to get her out of that cell tonight. His mind swirled with plans. He was a military man, he could figure a way. But could he convince her to trust him? He would.

***

Rayn was not allowed to eat with the other prisoners. What little food was offered, she ate alone in her cell. A rumble of voices came down the walkway. It gained volume until Rayn could hear the women in the cell next to her.

"Hey, lady. You Rayn?"

Rayn rose to her feet slowly, moving to the cell door. "Yeah?" She placed her arms through the bars.

"You know you up for execution?" The woman said it with hardness in her tone.

Rayn grabbed on to the bars to keep from falling. "I'm what?"

The woman laughed, shouted back down the line. "Good one! She didn't know!" Laughter echoed down the walkway.

Rayn leaned her forehead against the cold steel bars. *This could not be possible.*

Sensing a presence standing next to the doors made her look up into the eyes of Lieutenant Konner. She shrank back from him. He motioned the guard to open the door. Stepping in, he leaned back to the guard and whispered. The guard nodded, stepping away from the door. Rayn backed up until she was touching the wall. Draven kept his eyes on her face as he moved to her. Coming up to her, he leaned his hands against the cement wall, trapping her with his body.

Rayn watched him her mind not quite buying it.

Was he here to take her to her death?   Was he to be her executioner?

He leaned close to her, his warm breath spoke the words. "I have to get you out of here, tonight."

"You?" She spit at him.

A sigh escaped his lips. "Yes, me."

A thin smile curled her lips. "Yeah right." She edged away.

He grabbed her arm, hauled her back to him. "Listen. I'm all you have right now."

"No, I have others."

"Can they get you out of here?" His question deserved an answer she didn't have.

She didn't answer.

"I didn't think so. Now, I have a plan. I can get you out of here at midnight, but you must do as I say."

Snapping at him. "And if I don't?"

"Then tomorrow they **WILL** kill you. What have you got to lose by trusting me?"

Her eyes turned to look at the sincerity in his face. She couldn't decide if he was being straight with her. It could all be a ploy to gain her trust so she would give him access to the children.

But he was right. What was her other choices? If he were setting her up to be killed, it wouldn't make any difference.

She nodded. "Tell me what to do." She felt his body relax.

Was he really here to help her?

"Stay alert. I'll be here at midnight."

Rayn took hold of his arm as he move away from her. "And you have a plan?"

His eyes flicked at her. "Yes. Trust me Rayn. Please."

***

Rayn lay on her cot waiting for midnight, try as she might, another plan did not show itself. She had thought about Lieutenant Konner's offer, decided it was the best one she had. If he at least got her out of this building, she might have a fighting chance to run and get back to the farm.

A dark shadow passed across the cell doors. She had not even heard the footsteps. Lieutenant Konner unlocked the door with no sound. Immediately she went to him. Taking her hand, he led her along the darkened walkway, down the stairs, through a battery of doors. Each one he unlocked silently opened. She expected to hear alarms, but his skill moving through them to the outside amazed her.

This is almost too easy.

Once out of the building, a cycle waited for them in the alleyway next to Fort's exit. Throwing her a leather jacket and a helmet, she quickly put them on. He was on the cycle, she placed her hands on his shoulders, climbed on behind him. Her arms encircled his waist, her chest pressed against his back.

They took off at a great speed. The cycle was silent, implying a silencer had been installed. The wind broke across her face as the Fort moved away from them, as if parting to let them pass. The landscape was familiar but not the direction she expected. They were going west, her farm was south. But she wasn't going to ask questions now. She was waiting to see how this played out. Having been in tougher spots, for now, she was out of prison. That was a plus. And Lieutenant Konner was no match for her, even if he thought he was. Just being free was a feeling of redemption.

After about an hour, Lieutenant Konner guided the cycle up a small hill to a hidden cave, tucked behind a large bush. Ducking their heads, they moved carefully through the tunnel. The headlight shone down an endless shaft. A dark, damp feeling surrounded her. When they were hidden from the opening, he stopped. Balancing the large vehicle, he waited until she was off. She stepped aside and watched him park the cycle next to a stone wall. Returning, he kept his distance.

She stood with her hands in her back pockets. "What now, soldier boy?"

"We wait." Draven faced her, shrugging off her remark.

"For what? Until General Bono gets here?"

His eyes flicked in the darkness. "You still don't trust me."

"Not completely. But you did do what you said and got me out of prison."

"Fair enough." He crossed over to the other side of the cave.

She watched him with slight amusement. He kneeled to light a solar flame heater. How it was there and ready to be used made her think he had planned this for a while. When he looked up, he answered her unspoken question.

"I set this up today after I heard of the execution." He spread a heat blanket over the dank ground.

Rayn shuffled her feet as she moved toward the warmth of the heater. He stood, stepped backed as she moved in front of him. Lingering for just a moment, he then moved to a sack he had taken from a backpack.

Opening it, he threw her a sandwich. "Hungry?"

Rayn caught the bag in mid-air. "Yeah."

"Then eat." His words short and to the point.

Rayn sat cross-legged down on the blanket, keeping the cold ground away, took a big bite of the sandwich. He walked over handed her a cup of coffee. Nodding her thanks, the aroma filtered up as welcome as a friend. He sat opposite her with the flames between them. The sparks flickered in front of his face giving him a serene glow.

She felt her body relax, probably the first time in days. Her eyes got heavy. Fighting the sleep that threatened to overtake her, she still didn't trust him completely.

Maybe he is just waiting for me to pass out so he can tie me up. Force the truth about the children out of me.

Swaying with exhaustion, she felt him at her side, moving her body down to his coat for her head. Unwilling, her body stretched as he covered her with a rough wool blanket.

"Sleep, Rayn. I'll keep you safe."

His words made the doziness take over as she fell into a deep sleep.

***

When Rayn opened her eyes, she took a moment to adjust her eyes before she sat up. Looking around, taking in her surrounds, her mind clicked as to where she was and why she was here.

Pulling herself up, she pushed her hair from her eyes. Lieutenant Konner stood over by the stone wall. Removing his shirt, he displayed a back of ripping muscles and velvet skin. Rayn's eyes lingered as they moved down his back. Suddenly her eyes stopped, widening. On his back was a perfect square. She stood up, walked over to touch it. It was raised but smooth. As he felt her touch, he leaned back and smiled.

"What is this?" Her voice held a tone of alarm.

He looked over his shoulder where her touch rested. "It's a chip. Everyone gets them."

"No, they don't. I don't have one. What's it do?"

"It just identifies us ..." She saw the realization cross his face.

Rayn finished his sentence. "...and tracks you?"

He faced her. "I don't know. It might."

She took the knife from his waistband.

Grabbing hold of her hand, his voice held panic. "What are you going to do?"

"Cut the fucker out." Her voice calm.

"Whoa, wait a minute..." He raised his hands, backing away from her.

"Can you cut it out?" She lifted one firmly arched eyebrow.

"Well, no. I can't reach it…"

"Okay, then I'll do it." She spoke with the ease of one buttering toast.

"Is it necessary?" He eyed her skeptically

"Do you want them to find us?" She gave him one long searching look.

"No." His words came out firm, non-changeling.

"Then it comes out. Turn around soldier boy, grab the wall."

Draven took a deep breath, turned around placing his hands against the cold damp stone, braced himself. She moved the knife over the open flame. Carefully, she cut one small slit across the square. Sticking the point of the knife into the chip, she ripped it out. He winced, arched his back, but didn't make a sound. She dropped the chip on the ground, stomping on it. Reaching down, with her hands she dug a little deeper, took a handful of mud from the cave floor. Placing her hand on the wound, she applied pressure.

Draven looked back over his shoulder as she moved her hand over the wound. "What are you doing?"

"Healing you. The earth will heal you." When she was satisfied that the bleeding had stopped, she slapped him on the butt.

"There now, that wasn't so bad was it?" A cocky grin turned up her lips.

He turned from the wall, throwing daggers looks at her. "You enjoyed that." He snarled.

She turned away so he couldn't see her face, chuckled silently. "No, of course not." Turning back to face him. "What's the plan, Lieutenant Konner?"

He walked over to stand in front of her, removing his hand from his back. "Could you call me Dray? I think we are well passed the Lieutenant Konner phase."

"Why, Dray?"

"It's my name."

Rayn cocked her head. "Really? I guess I never thought of you having a first name."

His eyes showed that he was not amused.

She stopped baiting him. "Ok, Dray. What are we going to do now?"

He looked at his watch. "Well, it's well past noon. They are probably searching everywhere for you."

Rayn felt the panic go through her body with a shudder. "The farm."

"They probably went there first."

"No, we have to get there to make sure they are alright." Her urgency was replacing her logic.

He grabbed her shoulder to stop her shaking. "You can't have it both ways. You are involved in a fight. They will use and do whatever is necessary. If you can't handle the heat, get out!"

"You'd like that! Bring in the prize bitch. That would promote you up the ranks, wouldn't it?"

"I already had the prize bitch as you called it. If I want to move up the ranks on your back I would have left you there to be executed."

His word stung. But, he was right. If it was a trap, he had more than enough opportunity to have her caught. She searched his face. He kept his eyes on her, his hands still held her arms. She felt the overwhelming weight come full force on her shoulders. Her legs buckled, he went down to the ground with her, pulling her head into his naked chest, holding her tight.

"Rayn. Listen to me. We have to move to a safer place. I have a place about twenty miles south of here. We'll travel by night. The sun will set in about an hour, we'll leave then."

She pulled back to speak, but was afraid of the answer she would get from her question.

He nodded. "I'll find a safe way for you to contact them, but first to keep all of you out of harm's way, I need to get you away of the Cartel's radar."

**

25

Luna stood with Archer at the big window watching the troop of cyclists come into the yard.

General Bono's loud booming voice echoed across the valley. "Rayn!! Get out here Rayn!"

Hand in hand, they walked together outside. Luna drew herself up, speaking with a calm voice. "She's not here. You took her, remember?"

"Of course she's not!" He yelled at the men behind him. "Find her!"

Luna looked over at Archer and Galen, shrugging her shoulders.

Why didn't the general know where her mother was? If she was supposed to be with him and he is here looking for her, then...

Hope leaped up in her chest.

...she's escaped.

General Bono jumped from his cycle, stomped up the stairs. Pushing Luna and Archer aside, he barged into the house. He headed straight for the bookcase. Luna squeezed Archer's hand as they followed. General Bono stopped short, started stomping on the floor. The couple stood, watching him in amazement. His face was getting red, sweat beaded on his forehead. His soldiers came, gathering around him, as stunned as the others.

"What are you looking at?" His voice yelled at them. "There's a trap door here."

"Beg your pardon, Sir. But we have never found a trap door in all the times we have been here." One soldier ventured to tell him.

General Bono stopped his dancing around. His embarrassment was apparent to all who were standing around him. "Then...then...we'll take her daughter until she decides to come out of hiding with Lieutenant Konner."

"Lieutenant Konner? What does he have to do with Rayn?" Archer asked placing Luna behind him.

General Bono's startled expression turned to rage as he advanced toward them. "Don't pretend you don't know Lieutenant Konner took Rayn and now we can't find her."

"Took her where?" Luna pulled away from her husband's protection.

"If I knew that little lady, I wouldn't be here looking for her, now would I?" His breath was hot and sour on her face.

Luna pulled back from him. "Are you sure it was Lieutenant Konner?"

"I'm not sure of anything except she's gone spoiling my execution." General Bono turned away from the girl.

"Execution! You were going to execute my mother?" Luna's voice held fear for her soul.

Archer moved her behind him. "So Rayn got Lieutenant Konner to help her escape and now you can't find either one of them?"

The general stopped looked at his men. They were staring at him.

He turned sharply without answering the question. "Take her daughter, maybe then Rayn will decide to face her punishment." A solider grabbed Luna before Archer could react, dragging her outside, while other soldiers stepped up to grab Archer and Galen. Bono stopped quickly, looking down the stairs.

There stood twenty or more people waiting for him. Archer pulled himself away from the guards that held him, yanked Luna from the general's grasp, pulling her far away from him.

General Bono barked commands to his men as he stomped down the stairs. "Get on your bikes!" Once on his, he fixed his glaze on Luna and Archer. "If I don't find her I will be back for you. You can stand in for your precious mother!"

Luna and Archer stood on the deck until the sounds of the soldiers' cycles faded.

Luna darted back into the house. "Seth!"

27

Seth was already in the command room. "I can't get anything on her." He swirled around in the chair. "That's really a good thing. If I can't find her neither can they. She's well hidden."

"She's with Lieutenant Konner."

"What? Why is he on our side now?"

"I don't know. I don't know what to believe." She plopped down in the closest chair.

Archer came to her, took her hand, sat down on the arm of the chair. "He's right. Rayn has two things in her favor. They can't find her and Lieutenant Konner is good at what he does. We just don't know what he is doing with Rayn."

***

Lieutenant Milo listened to the outraged voice of General Bono on his phone. Sitting at his computer, he brought up the GPS of Lieutenant Konnor's chip. He felt like he was betraying a fellow comrade and a friend. It showed that Dray had traveled west, away from Rayn's farm. But General Bono insisted the two fugitives were there, so Lieutenant Milo stayed at the Fort waiting for a report.

Rubbing his temples, he listened to the commands from the General. "Yes sir. I will get a troop together and we will track the chip." The booming voice spoke on. "Yes, sir. We will find them."

Abruptly the phone went dead. Milo looked at the device.

Fine, I'll find them. You have wasted too much time just because you think you are right.

Transferring the data from his computer to his phone, Milo stood, walked around his desk.

Leaving his office, he shouted as he walked by two saluting men. "We are moving out."

"Yes sir." The two officers spoke in unison.

The hard soles of his boots clicked as he stomped down the hall, out the door. The bright evening sun blinded him for a moment until his eyes adjusted. Night would come soon. Before him was a company of about twenty-five men waiting on their bikes for his go ahead.

Hopping on his already running bike, Milo kicked up the guard, accelerated. Traveling down the main road in the Fort, the pack of soldiers passed by the dwellers of the Fort. Milo checked the coordinates, turning due west, he led the riders toward the spot that showed where Dray and Rayn were.

Following the dirt road for several miles, Milo noticed where the direction turned off, showing a line to a cliff in the hill. Milo held up his hands, stopping the squadron. Balancing his bike, Milo scanned the terrain. He could not figure out where the tracker was leading him. It said only a short distance and it stopped. Night had fallen an hour or so ago.

"Pierce." He spoke to the man next to him. "Pick a couple of men and follow me." Milo turned his bike toward the hill. Watching the screen, he followed the line leading him. At the bottom of the hill, he looked up. Squinting his eyes, he saw a narrow opening in the side of the cliff. A path led up to it, just wide enough to allow a bike. Bouncing over the rocks and potholes, he finally reached the opening, gunning his motor to jump up the last rut. Into the side of the hill he went. His headlight reflexed off the rock solid walls.

Then the light branched out, revealing a small open space. Milo cut his motor, secured his bike, walked around the area. The ground vibrated with the sound of the bikes. Milo frowned.

Someone had been here.

He kicked the embers left from the heater, saw the indention of a reclining body in the soft ground. Two sets of boot prints, one large, one smaller disturbed the powdery dust.

They had been here. But...

Pierce's voice interrupted Milo's thoughts. "Where are they?"

Good question.

Milo knelt down, picked up a hand full of dirt, let it run through his fingers. "I don't know." He stood turning completely around checking out the walls. "There is only one way in and one way out."

"What does the chip say?"

Milo chuckled more out of frustration than the humor of the situation. "It says this is where they are." He checked the signal again. It had stopped, flashing the words *this is your final destination!*

Finally, convinced that Rayn and Dray truly were not here and the only way out was the way they entered, Milo mounted his bike, driving out. Darkness settled over the land. Milo sat on his bike.

Where would I go if I was Dray?

He looked to the east.

No, that led back to the Fort.

West was a rougher terrain, it would be hard to cover with a cycle. And, since there was no abandoned bike, they must still be on it.

North or south?

It was a coin toss. In his gut he thought south.

So be it.

He started his engine, a sign that the others should do the same. Down the hill, he rode over the rough path until he reached the flat road. Heading south, the rest of his men followed him.

CHAPTER THREE

Dray pressed his cycle forward with expert ability through the heavy, dense woods. Over the rough terrain, his body shifted from side to side as they trekked over rocks and branches. Rayn, riding behind him, fit comfortably into his body. He felt her sway against him. He remembered holding her in the cave while she regained her composure. He still was not convinced she was fighting a worthwhile battle. But her conviction was so strong, he was amazed at the strength of her character.

Only a few more miles. The moon shone bright through the tree branches, giving them light. He first saw the outline of the cabin, his uncle had left to him. It was filled with childhood memories. No one knew about it. His father, uncle and mother were gone. So, he only came here alone when he needed rest or just the peaceful stillness of the lake. Early dawn broke over the lake as they approached the small dwelling. Rayn moved against his back.

"We're here." He spoke softly against her cheek. She repositioned her body to look around. He felt the rub of her jeans on his legs. A pleasurable shiver flooded his thighs. He groaned to himself.

Hold it together, man. She has more on her plate than you need to take on. Take on! I take on anymore and I'll burst from wanting her.

The large black motorcycle roared up to the front of the cabin. Stopping it in an easy, slow motion, Dray slipped off. His hand extended to Rayn to help her off. He kept all emotion from his face. He needed to remain neutral, uninvolved. When she tripped on the uneven ground, he steadied her at an arm's distance.

"Go on in." He needed to get away from her. He could feel a pull from her that was mysterious, dominant.

Dray pushed his cycle toward the garage, taking a moment to gather his thoughts.

I need to get her to a safe place.

He wished she would just stay here.

When he came back to the cabin, she had walked inside, standing in the middle of the room looking around. His cabin was neat and comfortable. Large quilts hung on the walls and over the furniture. It was small. One room had a space for the bed, a sitting area with a huge floor to ceiling stone fireplace, a small kitchen and a door that led to the bathroom. He walked around her, looking at her face. Her look told him she was pleased.

"What do you need?" His hands were in his back pockets, he wanted to touch her, but he held to his resolve.

She hesitated, turning around in a circle. "A bath, shower, something?"

He smiled at her discomfort, led her to the bathroom. It contained a huge tub and a separate shower.

"Take your choice. Anything else?"

"Clean clothes?"

He smiled to himself as he pointed to the closest. "Help yourself. Sorry that's all that's here.

"Thanks, that's fine."

He left her alone, closing the door behind him. Standing with his hand on the doorknob he heard the water run in the tub. He whistled as he went into the kitchen. He would take a shower later, right now, he was hungry.

***

As Dray came in from outside, he stopped suddenly when he saw Rayn. One of his shirts hung loosely on her curvaceous body. Her face glowed from the hot bath. He had seen and had many sexy women, but she looked sexier than any of them. He hoped his face didn't betray his lust.

"Hungry?"

"Yeah. What did you cook?"

He lifted the platter toward her. "Steak, potatoes, bread. Sit. Eat." His words were spoken as a directive instead of a request.

She moved to the table without an argument, took a chair. He filled her plate, stood back as she ate without talking. He noticed her eyes looked tired. As she slowed down her attack on her food, she leaned back, rubbing her temples.

"Go lay down." He softened his authoritative voice. Compassion was a new emotion for him.

Her eyes darted from him to the bed, then sharply back. A wry smile tipped his lips.

"I'll sleep on the couch. Go!" He waved his hand in the direction of the bed

Dray watched her as she got to her feet, went to the bed. His breath caught in his throat watching her curl up in the soft quilt, her eyes closed gradually. Sitting at the table for a long time, he wondered what to do now.

***

Rayn felt sleep fall away from her. Opening her eyes, she looked at the strange surroundings. As the memory of the last few days came back by degrees, she knew where she was and how she had got here. Lieutenant Konner had astonished her. His assistance in her escape from prison made her feel they were working together. This man, who had been the thorn in her side, was her collaborator for now.

How far should I trust him?

For right now, she had to do as he directed her. But her main object was to get back to the farm to make sure everything was safe.

Slipping out of the bed, the shirt she was wearing felt silky-smooth against her skin. His smell on it filled her senses. As she stood, the shirt fell down her body to her knees.

Good thing Lieutenant Konner was tall.

Rayn had only put on the shirt, her clothes needed to be washed as she had lived in them for three days. Following the scent of fresh coffee, she walked to the kitchen area. Passing the couch, she saw the untidy heap of the blanket and flattened pillow. She smiled, true to his word, he had slept on the couch.

Where was he, anyway? The cabin wasn't big enough to lose someone.

Rayn pushed her hair back from her face. Finding the coffee pot, she poured the delightful brew into a large cup. The blend of hot, strong liquid melted down her throat.

Her thoughts then focused on finding her clothes. As she entered the bathroom, looking around, they were not where she left them. Aware of a low, rumbling sound, she saw the washer and dryer in a corner. The colors of clothes rotated across the round glass in the dryer. She heard a slight movement behind her. Turning, she saw Lieutenant Konner sitting on the deck outside. Walking back through the kitchen, she grabbed her cup of coffee, went to the door, pushed back the screen.

***

Dray looked toward the cabin when he heard the screen door open. He sucked in a breath as his eyes took in the body of Rayn. Her hair messed, her face radiant from sleep, she presented a mental picture to him of soft breasts and curves under the simple shirt. Forcing his eyes back up to her face, he cleared his throat before he could speak.

"Good day." Keeping it unemotional, he hoped.

She walked over to the chair next to him, sat down. "What time is it?"

"Mid-morning." His eyes traveled down her shapely legs. Again, he shifted his eyes back to her face. She was looking out over the lake, the sun casting a shining luminosity across her face.

"So, lieutenant 'I-always- have-a-plan', what's your plan now?"

He looked away from her. This was the question he was dreading. "I don't know."

She jerked quickly to look at him with unexpected surprise. "You don't know? Great! I have things to do and you don't have a plan."

"And what do you have to do?" His voice raised in anger. Keeping her alive was his only thought.

Screw a plan.

34

"Get home! I need to be sure everything is okay." He couldn't believe how tunnel vision she was.

Lifting his cup to take a drink, he fought hard not to explode at her persistence. "Not a good plan. You will only bring the Cartel down on them."

He could felt the ire starting to rise in her. He had witnessed it too many times before. He didn't want to fight with her. On the contrary, he really wanted . . .

Her words were stinging. "You think he hasn't already been there?"

Calm. Stay calm.

He directed himself. "I'm sure he has, but if they find you there, they'll burn the house down. And..." he held her gaze. "...they will hurt the children."

Her silence told him that she had not completely come to trust him with the confirmation of the presence of children. She shifted her eyes away.

He studied her face. "You still can't admit you are hiding children."

She shook her head, speaking with a heavy resolution. "There are no children."

He didn't understand. But then he didn't have to. It wasn't his fight. "Well, us going to the farm is out of the question."

"Us? Who said anything about us?" She stood up, glared down at him. "I'm going, whether you like it or not. Just point me in the right direction. I have no idea where the hell I am."

"No." He looked back out at the lake, half expecting her to smack him.

"No?" Her voice rumbled like a small earthquake as she bent down to him. "Fine! I'll figure it out for myself!" She stomped back into the cabin, stopped at the door, shouting back over her shoulder. "Where the hell are my clothes?"

He jumped up from his chair, advancing toward her. Brushing past her, he spoke through clenched teeth. "I'll get them." His body touched hers slightly, she coiled back.

Her voice shouted behind him. "Look, solider boy, I know you don't understand what I am all about, but I have to do what I have to do!"

He twirled around to face her, placing his hands on the table standing between them. "No, I don't. I saved your sweet ass and all you want to do is put it back in danger. I am not going to help you do that!"

"Then I will do it without your help. You chose to help me get out of prison, avoid the execution. I didn't ask for your help." Her ungratefulness raised his temper to boiling.

Abruptly, Dray banged his hands on the table. The anger made the muscles in his neck throb. His blue eyes were dark with rage. "Enough! I'm done trying to explain this to you. They will kill you."

Rayn glared back at him. "That's not the point!"

He put his hands on his waist, mocking her movements. "And what, pray tell, is the point?"

Her body leaned toward him with an 'in-your-face stance'. "I have a mission..."

"Fuck this! I'm taking a shower to cool off." He threw his hands up in the air,

Dray stormed into the bathroom, slamming the door. He stopped in the middle of the room, ran his hands through hair. He was so mad he wanted to hit something. Going with his original plan, he turned the shower on full force.

The hot water made a steamy fog flow over the glass doors. Pulling his shirt over his head, he threw it in the corner. Unfastening his pants, he kicked them aside. Stepping into the shower, he leaned his hands on the wall, keeping his arms straight. The water beat down on his back, pounding his shoulder muscles.

The shower door flew open. Rayn was yelling. "You have no idea what we are about. I will to do this with or without your help."

Suddenly she stopped, as the realization that she was talking to a naked man flashed across her face. He watched as she became aware that she was staring. Her gaze skated over his bare chest, then lower. She dragged her eyes back up to his face.

Dray had not moved, he looked at her with a cocky smile. When she met his look, he felt an involuntary tightening low in his gut. She started to shut the door when he moved quickly. Stopping it with one hand, he grabbed her around the waist with the other. He backed her up against the shower wall, capturing her with his hardened body.

He groaned beneath his breath, settled his mouth on her lips. His tongue force her lips open as he brought her hips into him. When he felt her respond, he removed the wet shirt from her. He lifted her up and carried her out of the bathroom to the bed. Tossing her down, he pinned her beneath his firm, aching body.

His hands traveled up her, gently stroking, caressing, and fanning the flames he'd created. As his fingers moved to her side, down over her thighs, he closed his eyes, savoring the exquisite feel of her. He licked the side of her breast, inhaling deeply the scent of her skin. She moaned and squirmed. He could feel her going into ecstasy spasms as he moved on top of her. Holding just above her, he watched as she closed her eyes, her hands gripping the blanket. He thrust inside her as her moan turned to a scream. The intense and powerful thrust made her arch to take in more of him. He saw sweat beads in the hallow of her throat. Sucking the drops off, the sweet salty taste melted on his tongue.

He was a master at giving women pleasure, but this time his gratification was more than he had ever known. He felt her climax build, sensed his passion rising to its peak in unison with hers. Climaxing together, he stayed inside of her, relishing the feeling of completeness. When he rose up to look at her, she had tears on her cheeks.

He was alarmed. "Did I hurt you?"

She shook her head. She tried to speak but the words were silent. He removed himself carefully, sat back on his legs.

Rayn?" His voice was full of worry.

She raised her arms to cover her eyes. An indigo blue, spiky, tattooed crest encircling her upper left arm. It made him think of a lightning bolt. He touched it, it was cool to the touch, were as the rest of her skin was warm. "What is that?"

Murmuring under her arms, she didn't act like she was upset he had found it. "It's a symbol of the power. We all have them."

He didn't understand. "We all. . .?

"The righteous warriors. We receive them when we receive the power." Lowering her arms, she gathered his face in her hands. "It's part of the whole scheme of things." She left it at that.

Dray shook his head.

Nothing major, just tattoos that have their own temperature, the 'power', the warriors, righteous no less.

Using his thumb to wipe away her tears. "Why are you crying?"

She wiped the rest away. "It's not anything you've done, it's me."

"What have you done? Other than..." His tongue-in-cheek smile creased his eyes.

She put her hand over his mouth. "Shhh."

He took her ring finger in to his lips, sucking. Her eyes stayed on his, but her look was not of anger, or displeasure, but of satisfaction.

"I'm sleeping with the enemy." She laughed lightly.

The relief that flooded through him let him see the humor of the situation. "Trust me honey, that wasn't sleeping."

Her laughter shook her chest. It was the first time he had heard her laugh. He liked the sound. Smiling, he pulled her up to a sitting position. Wrapping her in his arms, he kissed her slowly, deeply, with a yielding hunger. She put her arms around his neck, pulling his head down.

Dray had a feeling wash over him that was unfamiliar, but delightful. He wanted to kiss this woman forever. The thought that she would ever leave his life was unbearable. He pulled back.

He knew what he had to do. "I'll get you safely to the farm."

She drew back in disbelief. "Why now? Just a minute ago, you were against it. I presumed I would have to fight you to let me go."

I'm not letting you go. I'm going with you. I understand your determination."

Her voice held a tone of enthusiasm. "You're joining us?"

Didn't say that. I'm just not your enemy."

She hugged him, giving him the feeling she was extremely pleased with his decision. He just hoped it was one he could live with.

CHAPTER FOUR

Dray finished his shower after Rayn had washed off and left to get her clothes. Lost in thought, he was baffled as to why he had agreed to take her back to the house that would probably be a trap. As he rubbed the washrag across his shoulders, he felt a small bump.

The chip Rayn had removed!

It was totally healed.

How could it heal that fast?

He remembered the pain as she had dug it out of his skin. Turning awkwardly, he looked over his shoulder, could see only a slight scar. This woman had powers he could not grasp. Plus, she had a grip on him, he didn't understand. No woman had made him want to do what he knew he shouldn't.

Join the Insurgents? No way! Support her cause? Not going to happen. Make love to her again? Gawd I hope so!

Stepping out, he dried himself with the towel, he kept thinking about what to do. By the time he wiped the steam from the mirror, he knew what he was going to do. He would take her to her house. Leave her with people that would keep her safe, return to the cabin to wait until all this blew over. It would. Things always do. Pulling his pants on, he slipped a shirt on and did not button it. Walking out of the steamy, hot bathroom, he felt the welcoming breeze of the cool wind from the lake. Rayn was standing against the rail of the deck. His plan was to approach her, but to keep his distance, explain his plan.

Leave her and go.

She turned at the sound of him coming through the door.

His resolve melted "We'll leave at midnight. It's about two hours. We'll get there just before dawn."

Redressed in her clean clothes, she was a stunning-looking woman. She leaned against the railing. "Are you sure you want to do this?'

No!

"Yes, I want you back safe with your people."

Keep it straight.

He watched as her expression changed from the hardened warrior to a calm, but in control woman. "Thank you. I'm sorry I was always so mean to you, but..."

I know. I was just as bad. We will get on with this then I..." Her eyes stopped him.

Will leave you?

"...figure it out as we go." With that, he turned away from her, walking back into the cabin. He sat down on the couch, buried his head in his hands. A soft touch on his back only further confused his conflicted feelings.

Dray." A voice like a soft breeze caressed him. "Talk to me."

I can't." He jumped up away from her, away from her touch, her voice that drew him in like a bee to honey.

Her eyes narrowed. "What?"

I can't leave you. I want to. I know I should, but I can't." His body slumped, she moved to him. Her arms closed around his waist. He gathered her to him. Not in a sexual way, but in a core-searching way that told him his soul would die if he left her.

She whispered softly against his neck. "It will work out. You will do what you must. We are meant to be together for now."

He begged her for an answer. "How do you know that?"

Her voice vibrated against his chest as if it was the words would solved all problems. "I know, because your spirit is bonding with mine. It happens. It's okay."

He pulled back, still touching her, he had a strange feeling that she was connecting with him. He didn't know if he liked it or even wanted it.

Then again, he wondered if he had any choice. "Glad you think it's okay." Resigning to her ways, his mind went to the plan. "We need to sleep if we are going to ride all night." A slight smile turned the corner of his mouth. "Can I sleep with you in the bed? This couch is killing me."

Yes." She took his hand. "But this time we sleep."

Sure." His voice carried a small hint of amusement, a small hint of a challenge.

***

Dray woke her with a soft kiss on her lips. She stirred slowly, her eyes opened with a smile in them.

"We need to get ready to leave." He told her in a honeyed whisper.

She nodded, rising easily. He took her hand, pulled her from the bed into his arms.

Nuzzling her neck, he whispered. "Are you sure we need to leave? We could stay here forever. No one would ever find us."

She laughed against his shoulder. "Wish I could." Her voice held a touch of regret.

Moving out of his arms, as she left him he felt an emptiness that made his heart ache.

Yeah, you're going to let her go, old boy!

When he walked to the kitchen area, she was leaning against the counter. He went to the duffle bag on the table, keeping his eyes away from her.

Putting food and supplies in the bag, he talked to keep from thinking. "It will take us about three hours to get there. The night is clear so we have the moonlight to help us see..."

Her voice cut through him, sparking an alarm. "Do you have any weapons?"

He raised his eyes to look at her. "Some. What do you want?"

"Whatever you have." Her voice was steel cold.

"Do you know how to use anything?" He raised an eyebrow to observe her reaction.

"Most. How old are you, Dray?"

Her question caught him off guard. "Why?"

"Just wondering. So?" She was looking at him over her coffee cup, her eyes waiting.

"Twenty-seven. Old enough?" His voice dripped with resentment.

"Gawd!" She whistled under her breath. Shaking her head, she moved over to look in the bag. "Put in whatever you have." Her eyes caught his in a holding embrace. "We'll need to be prepared."

"How old are you?" He asked pointedly.

A smile played at her lips. "Old enough." She turned to move away when he caught her by her arm.

He was now serious, he wanted her to see the whole picture. "Does our age really matter, considering what we are about to face?"

She looked deep in his eyes, concreting his resolve. "No, it doesn't"

***

Dray cut the motor on his bike, letting it slow on its own. Rayn tightened her hold on his waist.

"Sh-h-h." He whispered back to her. He slipped off the cycle effortlessly. She followed him where he was crouched by a large rock.

Reaching up, he pulled her down next to him. "Get down."

His words were spoken with authority. She couldn't see what alerted him, but she followed his directives. He pushed her gently to the ground, next to the rock. He crawled back to the bike, removed two guns. He held one out to her. His expression asked if she could use it. She nodded.

His panther-like movements amazed her. He was quick and soundless. As he took a position next to the rock, she moved up behind him, touching his back. Looking over his shoulder, she felt before she heard or saw the troop of motorcycles moving slowly across the meadow. His body tensed under her hand, she felt his breath come in long inhales.

Quietly she huddled against him, waiting for him to tell her what they were going to do. She hoped the troops just went by without finding them. Her fear was pounding in her head. Her breath was shallow and painful in her chest. She never quite got use to the fight. Sick dread coiled in the pit of her stomach. But she would fight, taking down whatever or whoever got in her way to get to the farm.

Waiting for his direction, she listened to the cycles echo across the valley. There must have been only five or so. They could they handle them. If they were captured, Bono would have them killed.

No, better to die here than at the hands of the mad man.

The troop stopped about a hundred yards from them. The leader looked around. Rayn recognized him as Bono's second in command, Lieutenant Milo. She felt Dray's intake of breath. Rubbing her hand down his back, she could feel his muscles tense, his body wired tight like a bowstring. Her head was close to his, she waited for him to speak. He didn't.

Lieutenant Milo raised his hand for quiet. He looked over toward the rock. Rayn prayed that the darkness would hide them. Her fingers closed tightly around Dray's arm. He stayed, still and strong as a statue. Her throat felt as if it was closing shut. Drawing on his strength, she held her breath. When she had to breathe, she let it out slow and silently.

His body ready for battle, she felt the fight rise in him. She bowed her head, leaned on his back. Steadying her shoulders, she closed her eyes in a silent prayer. After a moment, she raised her chin up. Side by side, they would stand up to the attack.

Milo called out. "Lieutenant Draven Konner!" His voice echoed across the valley. Dray did not answer. The silence radiated back.

"Dray." Milo's voice took on an 'I'm your friend' tone. Rayn wonder if Dray would believe it. He didn't respond, keeping his gun ready to fire. Her gun was at her side, cocked and ready.

"Sir?" A voice asked behind Milo. "Is there someone out there?" The young soldier's voice held a fearful tone he couldn't hide.

His words were drowned out by the clash of powerful thunder. A massive bolt of glaring lightening hit the ground between Milo and the rock. The Milo dug his heels into the ground, while he grabbed the handle bars to keep from falling off. The other four soldiers backed away from where the brilliant lightening had struck. Another intense bolt struck behind them, beside them, in front of them.

The sky roared like an angry animal as the violent sound shook the ground. Dark, foreboding clouds came low toward the group of frightened men. The moon had surrendered the sky's outburst that rolled across the land. More streaks of strong electrical fingers licked at the ground behind them. Huge drops of water fell, stinging the skin it touched. Yells and screams were heard as the men turned their cycles, gunned the motors, fleeing the storm.

Droplets hit Dray and Rayn, but they were soft, refreshing, like a lover's kiss. Dray stood up to look after the men running away from them.

"What just happened here?" He turned to look at her, skepticism in his eyes.

Rayn shrugged. "It rained." She hoped he accepted her simple answer.

"Noooo." He bore his eyes on her until she looked away from him. "The sky attacked them."

"Don't be silly! They weren't attacked. They were caught a flash thunder storm."

Taking hold of her left arm, he stared at the bright, flashing, red light that glowed under her shirt sleeve. She didn't have to look at it to know what it was showing. The next question was predictable.

"What is this?" His voice portrayed his disbelief.

She looked at his downcast eyes. "My tattoo. You saw it before."

He still had not taken his eyes off of her upper arm. She watched as the mark stopped blinking, turned black.

His grip lightened up, she let her arm drop to her side. She braced for his next question. "It changed colors?"

Easily, she removed her arm from his grasp, preparing to walk away before he asked the questions she didn't want to answer.

"The colors?" His insistent voice sounded behind her.

Rayn kept walking. "Yeah, it does that."

He came up behind her. His body heat felt like an energy that would suck her in. Smiling, she walked over to his cycle. Her body turned away from Dray, she lifted her thumb to the sky, mouthed the words 'thank you'.

With her helmet in her hand, she turned to see his silhouette in the darkness. As he came closer, she gazed at his chest covered in a wet shirt that clung to his rigid body.

Yeah.

She rubbed her left upper arm.

***

It was just before dawn when they came over the hill and saw the farm. Rayn sighed against his back, feeling the same liberation from him. They had finished the trip with no problems. Her radar had been up and ready as they crossed the unfamiliar terrain, but after the strange rain, the moon had come back out, lighting their way again. Pausing for just a minute, he leaned back against her body. He felt warm and comforting.

"Okay, we make it. How do we get down there without getting shot?"

Her words were spoken with assurance. "They aren't going to shoot us. I don't think."

"You don't think?" The humor in his voice was refreshing. She hugged him, feeling the release of relief. She was home. No matter what happened, what they had to face, she was home. And he had brought her here. She would be forever grateful.

As they approached the door, a man emerged from the shadows. "It's me, Rayn." She said over Dray's shoulder.

"Ms Rayn!" The man's voice carried his joy. She slid off the bike. Dray followed her, not saying anything. The man looked past Rayn to Dray. He quickly looked back at her, his hand instinctively raised the gun he was carrying.

Rayn put her hand on the gun, lowered it. "It's okay." He nodded.

Rayn took Dray's hand, led him toward the house.

"Wait." Jerking her to a stop. "What are they going to think of me being here?"

She touched his cheek gently with her hand. "They'll accept what I say." She smiled. "Trust me."

Up the deck stairs, she led him, on into the house. As she entered quietly, she saw Luna curled up in a chair. Hearing the door open she looked up. Her face radiated pleasure and surprise upon seeing her mother. Jumping up, she screamed as she flew into Rayn's arms.

"Mom!" Her shouts brought Archer and Galen to the front room. They both stopped short, waiting with smiles of gladness on their faces. Rayn smiled at them, then she saw their eyes go to the person standing behind her. Luna moved away from her mother, backing up to Archer.

Her face showed shock and fear. "What is he doing here?"

CHAPTER FIVE

Dray stood still as the people of the house gathered in to the room. He knew they viewed him as the enemy.

Rayn explained his presence to her daughter and son-in-law. "He got me away from the Cartel. He is only here to deliver me back."

"And then what?" Luna's voice held a tone of mistrust. "He goes to General Bono and tells him you're here?"

"He won't." Rayn voice was firm, convincing.

All eyes settled on him. He looked at all the faces. He hadn't realized that there were so many people at the farm.

Where had they been when he came for the raids?

He had no words to say to them.

Rayn stepped back, taking his hand. Pulling him with her. "Can we get something to eat? We've ridden all night, through a thunderstorm..." she winked at him. "...we're tired, dirty and hungry. We'll tell you everything while we eat, okay?"

Leading him to the table, she motioned to a chair. He sat down heavily. He was exhausted and famished. Food, a shower and sleep, then he would leave.

Let Rayn and her band of Insurgents fight their war.

He knew his military career was dead. He would go back to the cabin, wait and see who won, then decide his next strategic move.

A plate full of food placed in front of him awakened his sense of hunger. He didn't wait for an invitation. He dug in, eating most of it in a matter of minutes. A large cup of hot coffee finished his meal. The hot liquid brought him back to life.

He paid no attention to the talk at the table. He caught bits and pieces, but it was mostly Rayn and her group catching up on what had happened since she was taken from them. Looking around the room, he felt it was different from when he raided it. Full of people, noise and life. He scooted back from the table, when a little girl walked by him. She stopped, crawled up on his lap before he knew it. Taken by surprise, he watched the sweet, angelic face as she put both hands on his face.

"Who are you?" Her voice was soft and sweet.

"Dray." He was amazed that she touched his heart so. He had never been this close to a child. He had been an only child, no cousins, not many friends. He had seen the children at the Fort. But they were expressionless faces, dressed in gray, following instructions.

"My name is Cassie. You are pretty."

He smiled. He had never been called pretty before. Cassie reached up, kissed him sweetly on the cheek, then climbed down. His eyes followed her, he touched his cheek. He could still feel her kiss. When he looked up, Rayn and the others were staring at him. He felt a chill go down his back. Looking from one face to another, he knew he had not won their trust. Rayn got up from the table, held out her hand to him. He took it, stood.

Addressing her followers. "Let us get some rest, then we'll work out the strategy. Bono will be back. Me being here won't be a good thing."

Dray followed her up the stairs into a large hall with two huge rooms off to each side.

"Bathroom." She motioned to the left. "Bedroom." She walked to the right. He stood, waiting. Feeling his discomfort, she made the decision for him.

"Take a shower, then you can sleep. It's mid-morning, but we've been up all night." She pushed him into the bathroom.

Once in, he removed the dirty, wet, smelly clothes. Leaving them on the floor, he entered the hot shower, lathered up. The soapy smell calmed his senses. The exhaustion swept over him. It took all his energy to leave the shower. When he opened the shower door, a pile of clean clothes was laying on the counter. His dirty clothes were gone. After dressing, he stepped into the hall, crossing over to the bedroom. No one was in the large room, but he decided to lie down on the bed. His body was aching from the hard riding and conflict of the days before. He didn't want to sleep, he had too much to think about. But he lost the battle and soon welcomed sleep.

***

Rayn had showered and changed in one of the other bathrooms. She was in the washroom dumping their clothes into the washer.

Luna walked up to her mom, watching her perform the household chore. "So Mom, how did he get you out?"

"It was amazing. Quiet, quick, we were out and gone."

Her daughter folded her arms across her waist. "Where did he take you?"

"We went to a cabin he has." Closing the washer door, she faced her daughter.

"How did you get him to bring you here?"

The memory of their lovemaking flashed across her mind, reliving the pleasurable sensations.

Clearing her mind, she responded. "I don't know. He just said he would bring me here." She finished her chore, then turned to face her daughter. "He's leaving. He doesn't believe in our cause, which is okay. He's not a bad man, just brain-washed by the Cartel."

"But he saw one of the children. Won't he run back to Bono and tell him? That would put him back in the good graces of the Cartel if he could prove there were children." Luna walked around her mother.

Rayn just knew he could be trusted, Luna did not. There was no way she could convince any of them that she and Dray shared a spirit.

"He won't." Rayn banked on her daughter's faith in her. Luna frowned. "I hope you're right."

Rayn spoke under her breath. "So do I."

They moved to the kitchen. Rayn was tired but she wanted to let Dray sleep. If she crawled into bed with him, it would create speculation. Plus, she didn't know if she could not respond to his body, the pull of her desires.

Getting another cup of coffee, Rayn and Luna sat at the big table alone, the quiet and the darkness surrounding them. Explaining to Luna how they had traveled the countryside avoiding the Cartel, of the strange thunderstorm.

Luna still questioned Lieutenant Konner's transformation to a nice guy. Rayn understood her concerns. They had so much to protect.

"I just know he is being transformed. Why and how, I don't understand yet."

Luna got up from the table. "I hope you're right. He could put all of us in danger."

Rayn went to her work area. Sitting down at her computer, she went through massive e-mails and reports connecting the Insurgent groups. Many heard she was dead. She reassured them she was very much alive and back at the farm. But she warned them. Things were getting bad, that they must take extra precautions.

Seth walked over to her. "I installed a new filter, just in case the Cartel was trying to break through."

Rayn was very grateful for Seth. A techno wizard he kept them safe and hidden as they communicated with other groups. For hours, she worked on reassuring her contacts that the Cause would go on.

***

The sunset brought dusk to the valley as Dray fought though the dream haze that carried strange images. The little girl Cassie filtered through the fog, pulling up emotions he had not felt before.

He stretched, felt the bed next to him. It was empty, the blankets not even disturbed. His disappointment that Rayn wasn't there brought him fully awake. He knew he was leaving, had to leave, needed to leave. This was not his fight. But his heart hurt at the thought of leaving her, of not knowing when or if he would see her again. Crawling out of bed, he saw his clothes clean and folded on the footstool. He changed, went to find the way downstairs.

Descending the steps, he saw Rayn curled up in a chair in front of the fireplace. The flames cast a glow around her. He wanted her so bad, but it was not the time or place.

Will I ever feel her body again?

Bending down, he touched her cheek with the back of his fingers. She stirred, opened her eyes. A smile lit up her face.

"Hey." Her voice smoky, full of sleep.

"Hey." His eyes captured hers. "I need to get going or I will never get away from here."

Rolling her head on the back of the chair, her eyes watched his face. "Why?"

Looking into the eyes of this fascinating woman, he tried to keep light. "Why do I need to leave or why will I never leave?"

"Both." She straightened up in the chair, searching his face for the answer.

He sighed, lowered his eyes, he took her hands in his. "I need to leave you now or I will never be able to leave you. Rayn..." He looked up, as he squeezed her hands. "...I am infatuated with you, I think I could, no I probably will, love you for the rest of my life, but we come from different perspectives. You won't come over to mine and I can't accept yours. We are at an impasse."

Her eyes softened, wetting at the corners. She nodded her head. "I know. I guess this is what is called two separate worlds. I will forever be grateful to you for getting me back here." She stood up, pulling him up with her. He drew her into his arms, taking in the last smell of her he would ever know.

His voice full of emotion. "Come with me to the barn?"

They walked together out into the cool night air. The warmth of her hand in his was a memory he wanted to cherish. He couldn't dare to hope that he would ever see her again. His foreshadow of the future was to someday hear the news she was dead. Either by the hands of the Cartel or in a battle. He couldn't watch her die. He needed to extract himself from the pain that would come when she was cut down. He had no disillusions she would survive this war.

His black runner stood proud and shiny when he walked into the barn. Patting it lovingly he took hold of the handlebars, pushing it out into the night. Rayn walked behind him. Before he mounted, he turned, took her in his arms. His lips came to hers with an urgency he never felt when he kissed any other woman. Her body responded as she moved against him. A strong groan moved up his chest to his mouth. He took her lips into his, kissing her with the sorrow he felt in his soul. Prying away from her, she buried her head in his neck.

"Godspeed, Dray." She whispered, her voice full of loss.

He couldn't speak. He just turned away, swung up into the seat. With one last look, he turned the runner around, riding away from her.

The hurt ripping through his heart almost caused him to double over. He had never felt such a sense of sorrow. Not even when his parents died. He had never loved anyone or anything enough to feel such pain. He didn't know if he would survive this. The stars danced across the sky as the full moon lit his way. The wind whispered across the ground and through the trees.

You are leaving a love you will never know again. Can you live with that?

CHAPTER SIX

Dray felt the heavy weight of doom on his heart. Tearing himself away from Rayn was the hardest thing he had ever done. The conflict in him made it hard to concentrate. His head knew the way to the cabin, or so he hoped, because he was riding with a broken heart.

As he rode across the long stretch of field, all of a sudden his runner stopped as if out of gas. Dray checked the gauge and the tank. Plenty of gas. He swung his leg off the runner. He had no idea why it had stopped. Stepping on the kick stand, he steadied it.

Lifting his face to the sky, narrowing his eyes, he felt the hairs on the back of his neck stand on end. Looking around he watched as the moon sent sparkles down across the rocks and trees that dotted the land.

As Dray looked to the west, a flash of light lit up the midnight sky. The shadowy outline that emerged in front of him was the familiar rock where he had hidden with Rayn. All of a sudden, the realization of where he was knocked him in the chest like a blow.

The lightning storm!

It had crashed and hit here where he stood.

He felt the ground under him shake. Trying to keep his balance, it knocked him to his knees. As he knelt on the dry, warm, ground, a strong, intense wind wrapped around his body. It felt like he was being held in an embrace. He had no need to fight against it. Instead, he let the comforting sensation cascade over him. A rush of peacefulness flowed down his body, making him tremble.

He prayed to a god he didn't believe in. "Oh, God!" His eyes searched the night sky. "Stop the pain. Tell me what to do. She believes in you, do it for her."

As if an answer, the sky opened up, sending a soft, welcoming rain down on him. The warmth stopped his shivering. Dray waited, his hands on his thighs. His face studied the ground in front of him.

I can't. This is your journey. The voice held no sympathy.

As he rose to his knees, he lifted his fist in a gesture of defiance to the sky. "What do I do? She has her purpose. I have nothing."

The sky answered with a soft roll of thunder. **What do you want from her?**

Dray sat back on his legs. "I want...I want her to love me back."

The thunder crackled. **She does. But she loves the children more. Can you accept that?**

He lifted his eyes to the dark sky. "Why does she love the children?"

The air splintered around him. **Because she answers to a higher cause. That of the future.**

Dray lowered his head, put his hands together, folding them in his lap. "Why can't I be part of her future?"

Why indeed? The answer came with a rush of clouds moving across the land. Low enough when he looked up, he thought he could touch them.

The wind released him. He felt as if it stood back awaiting his answer. He raised his eyes to the sky. The full face of the moon looked down on him. The stars formed a clusters like groups of people. The sky was dark, but clear. No lighting, no rain, no wind. The temperature was prefect, neither warm nor cold. Dray rose to his feet. He thought about leaving, getting as far away from whatever was happening to him as he could, putting everything behind him. Rayn, the Insurgents, the Cause, the Cartel. He wanted to return to his unfeeling, pain-free world.

His body and soul exhausted, he decided to sleep first. Going to his runner, he lifted his backpack from the rack. Taking the gear over to the rock, for some unknown reason it was his comfort place. Pulling out his heat blanket, he removed his wet shirt, threw it over the rock to dry. Removing his jeans, he dug another pair out of his knap sack. Laying out the rest of his clothes across the rock. The solar flame heater created a ring of light when Dray lit it.

Settling down next to the fire, his thoughts were filled with confusing images. He quit trying the figure out why he had heard 'the voice of thunder'. He was reflecting more on what it had asked him. Dray had never had a moment of reckoning, but he was sure he was having one now.

The still night air touched his bare chest, bringing back memories of Rayn's body touching his when they had made love. He could still breathe in the scent of her. Leaning his head back against the rock, he closed his eyes. His body remembered the passion he had felt with her. He could almost swear if he reached out, she would be there. His breath was labored. His head filled with images of pleasure and ecstasy. He knew in his heart of hearts if he never felt her again, he would cease to exist. Clenching his fists, he felt his muscles tense.

Then the breeze touched him again, whispered in his ear.

Take your time. This is important. Think it through.

His body relaxed. Sleep came upon him. He moved his body down to the bedding.

In sleep, he dreamed of Rayn, of fighting beside her. Feeling her strength intensified, his ability to see her cause, her drive. He saw her mission. It opened up for him like a book, explaining why her purpose was so important. He felt her pain, her sorrow for the children.

Children! Dray was surrounded by bright-faced children who grew before his eyes into young men and women. He saw them winning the cause, fulfilling the dream of freedom. The Cartel failed, removed from power and replaced by peace.

His body thrashed against the visions. He couldn't decide between what was real now and what remained to come. As the images unfolded across his mind, he felt every emotion the scenes produced. The one major vision that came the strongest was of Rayn. She moved through his dream as a prevailing force that remained firm.

Just before dawn streaked across the morning sky, a strong clap of thunder woke him. Bolting upward, his senses took a while to establish he was awake and not still asleep.

Talking to the air, "What?" He shouted at the sky. It answered with a soft rumble, like a snicker.

He got up and stretched. Looking around he could make out the images of his runner and the rock.

The rock.

It stood proud and solid mocking him.

As the aroma of the instant coffee awakened his senses, he sat back against the rock. The cold, rough surface stung his bare skin. He had not slept outside since childhood. He had come to enjoy his creature comforts, the rewards of following commands, moving up the ranks.

But this morning was probably the first morning he had woken up with a feeling of tranquility and exhilaration. Why he was so happy mystified him. He knew there was a higher purpose for his life, and it included Rayn.

Sitting against the rock, he watched the red streak of daybreak cross his horizon. The day unraveled bright and clear. His questions still circled his head, but he ignored them. There would be time to deal with them later. He knew this wasn't over, just a step at a time toward a solution.

He sat undisturbed for about an hour. Unaware of the change in the atmosphere, he was shaken to his core as a loud blast of thunder vibrated the ground. He rose quickly to his feet as a strong cold wind whipped around his naked chest. He grabbed for his shirt, but it was ripped from his hands.

The wind slammed his body against the rock. The rough edges cut into his back. Lightning struck to his left, then to his right. He recoiled against the rock. The sky was a menace of dark clouds rolling toward him. Illuminating flashes of light streaked across the sky. One hit just in front of him. He threw his arms over his face for protection. He could feel the heat from the lightening on his skin.

What was so pissed at him and why?

The thunder roared its answer. **Take a stand or leave her alone.**

Dray felt more than heard the words. His response was anger. "Why should I?"

Because she has a higher calling.

Dray was getting tired of this. "You told me that. Why can't I be her calling?"

The voice chuckled. **You are not worthy.**

Now he was pissed. "Who are you to tell me that?"

The answer came with a spirit of authority. **The high command.**

The words were spoken with a prevailing energy, pressing Dray back against the rock. He fought against the power. Prying his body from the rock, he fell to the ground, rolling away from the energy that held him.

Bouncing back on his feet, he raised his arms at the sky. "Stop! I am worthy of her."

The strong and commanding voice boomed across the air. **Prove it.**

"How?" He felt his will deflated. Trying to stand strong, the force of the words put him to his knees. He had nothing with which to defend himself.

With one last mighty blast against him, the voice came back. **Figure it out.**

The sky cleared to a bright blue. The wind stopped. The quiet was alarming. Dray stood, looked warily around. Moving slowly, with extreme caution, he collapsed on his bedding.

God, what the fuck is going on? Am I losing my friggin' mind?

Shaking his fist at the sky, he yelled. "Don't answer that!"

***

"Dray." The voice was silky and feminine. He stirred in his sleep.

"Rayn?" The hope leaped in him. She had found him. He forced his eyes open to look at only empty space. He shot up, looked sharply around, ran a hand through his hair. He had heard her. She was here, he knew it.

The day was giving way to evening. Dusk settled across a darkening sky. He buried his head on his knees. It had been twenty-four hours since he had left. He had been held captivate here, arguing with nothing.

I've had it.

He stood up, gathered up his gear, yanking his clothes from the rock. Going over to his runner, he loaded up his things. Picking his shirt up from the sandy ground, he shook it, glaring up at the sky. Then he put it on. Looking out at the horizon he dared it to stop him. But all he heard was a deafening silence. Walking to his runner, he murmured to himself.

"Done with this." He lifted his eyes to the sky. "If you're going to stop me, then just do it or give me one good reason why I should go back to the farm other than to die serving a cause I don't believe in."

Quiet.

"Fine, I'm out of here. Sound your thunder. Fire off your lightening. I am going to forget any of this happened."

He swung up onto the runner. When his butt touched the soft leather, he felt the warmth of Rayn's body against his. "Stop." He pleaded. "I can't help her. It goes against everything I know.

The wind touched his body like a patient lover. He groaned, threw his head back. His loins were warming and getting hotter. It was a mixture of desire and need. "You can't honestly be tempting me with carnal feelings?"

He felt the wind chuckle. It infuriated him. Whatever this experience was, he was not going to react to it anymore. He did not exist in this kind of world. His world was logic and strategy, not magic.

Turning his runner toward the cabin, away from the farm he felt confident he would escape any more episodes.

Then the voice spoke. **If you leave now, it will be too late to ever return.**

He stopped trying to start the runner. The voice had his full attention. "Why too late?"

Quiet.

"Damn it speak to me! Why too late?" His voice echoed through the valley, only to come back to mimic him.

Then he heard the low, steady tone of the voice envelop him speaking the words that chilled his very soul. **Only you can stop them from killing her.**

"Shit!" He said.

CHAPTER SEVEN

As the day turned to dark, Rayn walked out to the barn to check on her horse. Gently petting his nose, she whispered quiet words of comfort. Unaware of the dark shadow moving behind her, an arm encircled her waist, pushing her up against the stable wall. Another hand covered her mouth. The startled look in her eyes softened as she recognized the dark figure.

Dray!

Giving her a warning look, he slid his hand off her mouth to cover her lips with his own. As he relaxed his hold on her, he slid his arms around her waist drawing her to him.

Returning his kiss with all the pent up emotion of the past days, her memory returned to when he made love to her, the way her body responded to his every touch. Pinning her next to the wall with his body, he pulled back, looking at her with a smirk.

She hit him on the chest. "You scared the bejeebers out of me."

His next kiss was hard and deep. Her arms wrapped around his neck, returning his passion.

"Where can we go?" His voice deep, whispery.

"Up to the loft."

He took her hand, led her to a ladder. Allowing her to climb up first, Rayn waited at the top as he came behind her. She moved eagerly to his arms. Her passion for him rose up through her body as a fiery heat. With only a bare wood floor to lay on, he followed her down.

As if time did not exist, the sweet sounds of night serenaded them through the opening in the roof. As his tight, firm body moved over her, she caressed his back, allowing the feelings of desire to wash over her. His lips moved down her, tormenting her with his tongue. He took his time. There was still the rising need, but he made love differently. As if he was drinking her in, savoring the taste and touch of her.

Her eagerness rose up to meet his. This time she didn't allow the feelings of regret to stop her. She wanted this man. So, for now, she would permit her body and soul to feel his presence. Releasing a longing she had denied, made the lovemaking powerful and all consuming. He spoke against her breasts, sweet words of affection. Her body tingled from his breath on her skin. Moaning involuntary, she arched her body to meet him.

His words aroused a need in her so deeply hidden. "We have a great love to share. Give me all you have, Rayn. Don't hold back."

Her fingers grabbed hold of his head, running her hands through his thick, soft hair as his touch inflamed her. Knowing he had come back, come back to her, allowed her spirit to open up to him. She had kept it closed for so long, only focusing on the Cause. When her husband died, she accepted that she was to go it alone. But Dray had been sent into her life. Her attraction to him came almost immediately, but she fought it as she fought anything connected to the Cartel.

But the time to stop fighting him and embrace him was now. She needed for him to have all of her. Surrender was not easy for her. Standing strong for so long, it seemed like a betrayal of her soul.

The night wind whispered in her ear. **He has passed the test. Love him. It is your destiny.**

Ryan arched up to meet him. Her climax cascaded over her like a soft, but steady waterfall. Freedom allowed the ecstasy of the moment to fill every inch of her body. Fire and ice mixed together to bring her into one with this man.

This time he entered her slowly. Each thrust brought her to a higher level of bliss. When she felt his climax building, hers rose to its peak in unison with him.

Their bodies glistening in the light of the full moon, she clutched him to her. Wrapping her arms around his hard body, feeling his heart beat against her chest, they stayed together until they could breathe.

Afterwards, holding him, she wanted to crawl inside of his heart and stay where it was safe. Her embrace tightened as he increased his hold on her. The night stars looking down from the skylight reminded her that once the world made sense. She buried her head in his shoulder.

"Dray." She whispered his name, kissed his neck.

He laid his arm across his forehead. Sighing deeply, he held her hand. "Rayn, I love you."

She noticed the tattoo on his arm, the same as hers. Both were a bright, sparkling, indigo blue. Tracing it with her finger, the coolness was like a fresh snow. Refreshing.

Dray turned to look at where she was touching. "You're kidding. I am now one of the righteous?"

Rayn nodded.

Dray raised up on his elbow, facing her. "So now will you tell me what the colors mean?

"Red gives the ability and strength to fight. Black is neutral, but it supplies knowledge and mystical skills."

Dray touched the tip of her nose with his finger. "And blue is?"

"Sexual desire."

He chuckled. "That makes sense."

Rayn loved the pompous look on his face. "So what brought you back?"

His voice was deep and smoky. "You wouldn't believe...No you probably would. Lightening."

"You were at the rock?"

He pulled back, looked at her. "How did you know it was at the rock?"

She nestled down in his arms so he couldn't see her face. "Just a guess."

He placed his finger under her chin, forcing her head back to see her face. She sighed deeply and raised her eyes to his. "It really was a guess. What happened?"

"I had a close encounter of the booming voice, flashes of lightening kind."

Only imagining what had happened, she sat up, crossed her legs. "What did it tell you?"

A smile curled the corner of his mouth as she looked over at her. "You just accept it happened?"

"Yes. Now tell me about it."

"It told me I was the only one that could stop them from killing you."

"And you came back for that?"

His laugh held a point of relief. "Yes, that was what brought me back. I drove all night to get to you. I was afraid I would be too late."

She picked up his hand, held it to her cheek. "Whatever brought you back to me, I'm glad."

***

Without disturbing anyone in the house, Dray and Rayn sneaked through the rooms, up the stairs and into Rayn's bedroom. Wrapping Rayn in his arms, they slept together.

Dray awoke to empty arms, empty bed and empty room. Remembering where the bathroom was, he checked the hall, then crossed over. He had to smile when he saw the neatly folded pile of men's clothes waiting for him.

The hot, welcoming water washed away two days' worth of sand, rain and dust. A shower had never felt so good. Running the wash rag over his chest, around to his back, his mind wondered if he had any idea what he was going to do now.

Nope, no clue.

A spirit bigger than himself had guided him here. He would just have to trust it to steer him in the right direction. He knew for a fact he would not be doing battle with it again. It had made that perfectly clear. If he disregarded its direction, Rayn would be caught in a deadly trap.

Clean, dressed, he felt one hundred percent better.

Okay man, it's time to face the music. You have made a good, but unpopular decision. It will not be easy to stand on the convictions that a month ago you fought against.

Down the hall, to the stairs, he steadied himself with the banister. The mummer of low voices echoed up. Everyone must be in the dining area. Taking one slow step at a time, when he reached the bottom, he saw a large group people at three tables. Rayn sat with Archer and Luna at the first table.

Hearing his boots on the hardwood floor made her turn to look at Dray. He shrugged. The people on the room went silent. Galen was leaning against the back wall. Dray searched his face for some kind of expression.

Was he for or not in favor of Dray's decision?

For some unknown reason it mattered to him what Galen thought. He didn't really know why. But then there were a lot of whys he didn't have answers for yet. Galen nodded, giving Dray the encouragement he needed.

Rayn stood up and addressed the faces that were watching for her lead. "Mr. Konner is joining our group." A low mummer waved across the people. "He is no longer a lieutenant. His knowledge of the Cartel and his military training will be invaluable to us. His loyalty is with us now."

No one objected. This surprised Dray, but he was learning that the group fought over very few minor details. The big picture was more important.

As the crowd rose and moved away from the tables, Rayn, Archer and Luna stayed seated. She motioned Dray over. Just as he reached the chair, a young woman placed a plate of eggs, bacon and hash browns on the table for him, along with a large mug of hot coffee.

It took him by surprise. She moved swiftly away as he told her thank you. Galen came over to the table. The four leaders of the resistance smiled and nodded. Dray was surprised, but proud to be part of their pact.

***

After breakfast, Rayn and Dray walked the compound. Explaining to him, he understood now why he could never crack the shell. They were a strong force of people willing to stand together for one cause. He had never seen such strength, not even in the military.

67

"I'm impressed." He held open the wooden gate for Rayn as they walked from one pasture to another. Different animals grazed in each section. This was their food source. Going back to the basics, the Insurgents lived on fresh fruits and vegetables. Good protein sources of meat and milk.

"I had no idea you were this self-sufficient. Where was all this when I raided your farm?"

Leading him to an open space, she lifted a heavy door recessed into the ground. Someone who didn't know what they were looking for would have walked or driven right over it.

The stairway was barely visual. Rayn took a light from the side wall. Illuminating the dark pit, it showed the way down the stairs.

Rayn begin explaining the method used to hide when there was a raid.

"The animals are taken to a shed in the woods. Then the people come down here." She was leading him down a narrow cement block walkway.

"How did you get things hidden so quickly? We would just pull up in your yard."

He could hear her laugh in the semi-darkness. "Number one, you weren't that unpredictable, second we were warned."

But of course. Now he knew how. The voice. "Where are we? As in contrast to up above?"

"Under the barn." To his right, a stairway came into view. They passed on by. The walls were farther apart, making a wider walkway. Large rooms were now on one side of the hall. "This where the children are hidden."

Glancing in, Dray saw rooms filled with canned foods, water and blankets. They could hold up for weeks down here. A bomb could explode topside and the people in this place would survive. The next room shocked him. It was on the opposite side. Rayn stopped to let him walk in. No words could describe what he saw. Guns and weapons of all kinds. These people were seriously armed.

He turned to her. "You were ready for a fight."

Her eyes were deep with the honesty she wanted him to understand. "Still are. We don't want to fight. But we can if we have to."

Dray followed her out of the weapons room. Well, he knew if there was an all-out fight, they were well equipped.

Reaching a wide wooden staircase, Rayn pushed a button, the wall at the top opened as they climbed up. At the top was the huge gathering room of the house. They had come full circle.

Following the nice ass of Rayn, Dray's eyes adjusted from the dark of the cellar to the bright sunlight streaming into room.

Rayn pushed a button and the wall closed leaving an impression of a large deep bookcase. Dray had seen this wall several times. Chuckling, he had never suspected it was the doorway to the hiding place for the children.

"Come." Rayn instructed him to keep following her. The next room was his biggest surprise.

The tech room was quiet at the moment. The only two in the room were two young men watching vigil over the computers.

Rayn introduced Dray. "Seth, Edward, this is Dray or as we used to know him, Lieutenant Konner."

Seth jumped up. He was a happy little guy. His grip was firm and friendly as he shook Dray's hand. "So, you are no longer going to sweep down on us?"

Dray laugh. Funny guy. "No, I have been converted." He took a side-glance at Rayn, winked.

Edward was not as welcoming. His hand shake was weak, he pulled away quickly. Dray had learned a lot about judging a person by their handshake. Edward's disturbed him.

Rayn went on with her tour. "This is the hub of our operation. Seth is a techno wiz. He can track anyone, anything."

Dray eyed the two men. Seth prattled at a mile a minute, explaining everything to Dray. Dray was quite familiar with the workings of a highly sophisticated communication system. Even half listening, he understood what was being told to him. But his attention was on Edward, who avoided eye contact, turning his back to the three others.

When they walked out, Rayn stopped Dray when they were away from the room's door. "What's wrong? You are tense."

Dray looked back at the room's door, then back at Rayn. "Just a feeling. If it is something, it will show itself. Just a gut feeling

Rayn walked across the yard deep in her own thoughts. From behind a tree, Seth stepped out. It startled her, but she noticed the worried look on his face.

He blocked her path, looked around, leaned in and asked. "Are you alone?"

Rayn narrowed her eyes, nodded.

When he took her arm there was a roughness in his grip. "Walk with me. I have something to tell you."

Rayn allowed him to lead her down the walkway, behind the barn. Once out of sight, he released her, turning his back.

She sat down on a bale of hay, her hands on her knees. "Talk to me, Seth."

Without turning around, his voice was shallow and low. "We have a traitor."

His words hit like a slap on the face. She lowered her head, feeling the weight of the news bearing down on her shoulders.

Saying the words that broke her heart. "Who?"

Seth took a deep breath. His back still to her, he straightened up, his tense muscle pressed against his shirt. "I don't know."

Rayn was still shocked. "How do you know there is one?"

Seth turned to face her. His clear blue eyes were clouded with doubt. "I intercepted a renegade transmission."

Her arms still braced on her knees, she could feel the tension in her hands. "Where did it come from?"

"It used our hub. If it had gotten through, the Cartel could have traced it. Stopped all our communication." Seth knew the highway of the Internet as well as some know the road home. Rayn trusted his explanation.

Taking in a deep breath, she continued on. "What did it say?"

"Rayn and Lieutenant Konner are at the farm." With his last words, his eyes focused on hers.

Searching his face, she then pressed on. "Any idea who?"

He shook his head. "No, but it is one of our technical team. It came from the command room."

Raising slowly, she moved closer to him. Asking the question she hated to ask, she swallowed, braced herself for the answer. "Do you think it's Dray?"

His face went deep in thought. "Actually, no."

Her breath came out in a rush. "Why?"

"Number one, he's never in the command room. Number two, the message was 'Rayn and Lieutenant Konner are at the farm' not 'we are at the farm'. Just speculation but no I don't think it's him. Don't you trust him?"

The relief made her smile. "Yes, I do trust him, but I know a lot of people here don't. I had to ask. I had to be sure." Her voice took on the tone of a commander. "So, how do we find out who it is?"

"I'll send a bogus reply. Set up an isolated thread that is inaccessible. Tracking the times of transmission. It will show up on the log."

"Good. Keep me informed. Thanks for being on the ball." Slipping her arm through his, they started back to the house. She was grateful for Seth. He was one of those blessings that just showed up at the door.

***

The young man that stood before Rayn and her husband Heath kept his eyes on the ground. Sent by a reliable source, they knew everything they needed about him. All that was left was to set up the time for him and his family to enter the compound. His credentials included a technical knowledge that was second nature to him. Having someone that could handle all the communication and keep up with all the new hi-tech methods the Cartel was utilizing was a major asset.

Heath put his hand on the Seth's shoulder. "You are coming with your with wife and two daughters?"

"Yes, Sir." He looked up, searching the faces of the couple that stood before him.

Heath chuckled. "No sirs here. We are fighting to keep our children. That is our cause, our means for existing. If you agree with that, we will have your family to the farm by tonight.

***

"Fire!!"

The words gave Dray a gut reaction. Pushing the covers back, his bare feet hit floor with a thump. As he bolted for the door, Rayn was ahead of him. Archer and Luna met them at the top of the stairs. Together, they flew down the stairs, out into the cold night air. Roaring flames shot up from the barn. The sounds of frightened animals came from within. People rushed in to get to the confused stock. Water arched, pouring from a hose attached to the reserve well. Without thinking, Dray ran into the barn.

His feet, cut and bleeding from the rocks

He ran across on the driveway. He saw Rayn grab her horse. As her hands touched the out of control animal, he stopped fighting her, allowing her to lead him out of the barn. Dray took his eyes off Rayn, grabbed the first hairy skin he touched. It was the stubborn jack ass. Grabbing for his halter, the animal backed away. The look of pure terror in its eyes. Dray plunged forward, finally got a hold of the leather. Yanking as hard has he could he drug the reluctant animal though the blinding smoke, around the flaming beams that fell around them.

Once the jack ass passed the smoke, it kicked its back heels, jerking free of Dray's hold. Dray didn't stay to watch. He turned, went back in. One by one he lead various animals from the consuming fire. His chest hurt from holding his breath, trying not to inhale the deadly smoke. Keeping low, he worked beside the other people to rescue as many animals as possible.

Dray heard a crackle above him. Before he could look up, a flaming wooden beam fell next to him, the flames licked his side as it crashed. The impact knocked him to the ground. His body, weak from the strain of fighting the animals and the fire, he took his last bit of strength to push himself up.

A rush of cold water crashed down on him, forcing him back down to the ground. He lay there, letting his sore lungs breathe in the cool mist that surrounded him.

"Dray!" Archer's voice cut through the fog that threatened to overcome him. He felt Archer shake his shoulders, "Dray, are you okay?"

The strength it would take to speak was not available, but he did push himself up, turning his body to sit on the ground. Holding his head in his hand, he let it clear for a moment.

Archer was kneeling next to him. "You good?"

Dray's voice came out raspy, his throat dry, painful. "Yeah."

His hands braced him as he lifted his body from the floor. Water dripped from the few beams that had remained intact, hitting his skin with whip-like touches. Looking up, the night sky above him showed a large gaping hole. The area around him confirmed major damage had been done to the barn. Slowly, he moved his stiff and sore body toward the door.

Rayn was his first thought. The last time he saw her she was leading her horse out of the fire. As he went through what was left of the barn door, he looked around at the group of people working in the yard, their faces black from the ashes and grim of the fire. His eyes rested on Rayn, talking to Seth and Galen far away from the crowd. Their faces creased with concern. Not caring if he was intruding, he walked up behind them, coming in on the middle of their conversation.

"It was set, Galen." Seth and Rayn passed a look.

Galen caught the exchange. "What's going on?"

Dray's presence stopped the answer. Dray didn't care. He was here to protect Rayn and he was going to find out what went on tonight with or without their permission.

Rayn slipped her arm around his waist, drawing him into the circle. She spoke to Galen, "We have a traitor." His face radiated his shock.

Dray was also taken back. He kept quiet and listened. He had dealt with traitors before. They get cocky, they get caught.

"Who?" Galen's eyes searched the faces.

Seth gave the answer. "We don't know."

Galen, as did Dray turned their attention to Seth. "Someone is sending out messages to the Cartel. We've intercede them but, we don't really know who we are up against."

Dray drew Rayn close to him, waiting for the obvious accusation. Him. He was the outsider, the unstable denominator.

Galen looked over at the swarm of people. "Well, we will have to set a trap." He moved his gaze to Dray. "Dray, you've probably had to do that sometime. Think up a plan."

Dray was shocked by his request. He could only nod. He thought for sure they would have suspected him. The small group disbanded. Dray let go of Rayn, leaned toward Galen.

He had to ask the question. "Why didn't you think it was me?"

Galen let a small smile play at his lips. "Is it you?"

Dray narrowed his eyes to see if he was kidding. "No."

Galen slapped him on the back. "Well, there you go."

CHAPTER NINE

Rayn stood looking at the destruction of the barn.
How could someone do this?

The weight of disappointment crashed down on her. For ten years she had stood strong. Created a haven for the followers, then someone could destroy it all in a flash.

Thank God it was the barn not the house.

But why the barn and not the house?

"It was meant to be a signal" Dray's voice sounded behind her.

Rayn did not turn to face him. Instead she went stiff, stepping away from him. "A signal for what?" Anger didn't even begin to describe her feelings.

Dray walked around to look at her. She kept her stare straight, not looking at him. "To let Bono know we are here. Since Seth blocked the transmissions, it was an alternative."

Taking in a deep breath, Rayn smelled the disturbing odor of smoldering wood, the water soaked hay. Raising her chin, she narrowed her eyes. The sight of the destroyed building made her sick to her stomach.

Turning her head, she searched Dray's face. "What if it had been the house?"

Dray shrugged, looked toward the barn as another beam fell, crashing to the ground with a loud bang. Neither he nor Ryan flinched. "Next time it might be."

"Then we need to make sure there isn't a next time." Her eyes begged him. Then she said the words she had never said before. "Help me...us...find this person?"

Dray put his hands lightly on her shoulders. "I will. I have some ideas. Let me work this out."

His words brought her a sense of comfort. Walking into his arms, she pressed her face against his smoky shirt. "Okay. Just protect us. I couldn't stand it if something happened to these people."

Speaking against the top of her head. "I know. Nothing more will. I promise."

"That's a promise I will hold you to." Pulling back, she nodded. "Let's go talk to the others. We need to figure this out. And we need to do it now."

Rayn gave the barn one last look. The coldness in her heart caused a sharp pain. Turning on her heels, she stomped toward the house. Mad as hell.

The shit is going to hit the fan. Someone is going to pay for this!

Marching up the stairs, she yanked opened the door. Galen, Archer, Seth and Luna were sitting at the dining table.

Taking long strides, she reached the table, slapping her hands down. "What just happened out there?"

Galen cleared his throat. "Our traitor just got brave."

"Or desperate." Archer pitched in.

Rayn turned to Seth. "Talk to me Seth."

Seth pushed his black glasses up his nose. "I found three transmissions that were blocked today. I guess the traitor decided to send a smoke signal." He grimaced at her.

Rayn looked over at Dray, who had moved to the table, but was still standing. "How do we stop him or her?"

Galen looked up at Dray. "We set a trap."

Rayn frowned. "I thought we had done that?"

Dray shook his head. "No, we just aggravated them."

"Them? Do you think we have more than one?" Archer looked to Dray.

Dray shrugged. "Not necessarily. But...we should consider all possibilities."

Rayn straightened up. "So, what do we do next?"

Dray folded his arms over his chest. "First, we stop discussing it out in the open. We need a room that will provide protection from others' hearing."

Seth spoke up. "The control room."

Dray frowned.

Seth shook his head. "Not the one up here, there's another one."

"Where?" Dray was confused.

Rayn nodded. "It's only known to the five of us. No one will be able to penetrate it." She looks straight at Dray. "Next?"

"We need to set up night guards. People we absolutely trust."

Rayn looked at the group. "That will be us here. Pick an area folks. We'll make coffee, it will be a long night." She turned to leave, but looked back. "Anything else?"

Dray shrugged. "We meet tomorrow in your secret room." He looked around at the group. "We'll find out who is behind this." He stopped as he connected with Rayn's eyes. She felt the sincerely of his words.

This will end. Either nicely or harshly, but it will end.

She nodded at him, turned and walks away.

***

Rayn stomped up to her room. Her anger was consuming her whole being. The work she had put into protecting the children could be brought down by one deceitful person.

I will find the traitor and...

And what dear heart? Shoot 'em.

Walking to the window, she watched the people move about the yard, doing their chores, their duties.

Why would someone walk in here and decide to turn against us?

And how long had she trusted someone to only be betrayed?

The questions clawed at her insides. The years of preparation, then the stand against the Cartel. She thought everyone understood. They had to remain strong, together, no weak link.

Rayn leaned her head against the cool glass. Her mind searched for answers.

Who would I distrust?

She came up blank. Some of the people she knew well, but some barely and some not at all. The farm had about a hundred residents. They had started with four.

Heath. You left me to carry-on. I will honor you by doing just that.

The memories of the night that changed her life unfolded like a dream, turning in her mind.

***

Standing before her, Heath kissed her. Her husband was a gentle soul, yet possessed a strength that radiated. "It'll be alright."

Rayn felt a stirring in her spirit. "This feels bad. Well, not bad, just...not all good."

Heath's dark eyes looked confident. "It doesn't matter. I have to go. It's our calling. Galen will be with me. We took precautions to be safe."

Rayn knew the drill, Heath and Galen would be meeting a couple that wanted to join the Insurgents. But there was something different about this. The couple had powerful influence in the Cartel. While she didn't have their names, she knew they would be a good addition to the Cause. And that is what made it so much more dangerous.

Heath pulled her to him. She snuggled down into him. The steady beating of his heart told her he was in control.

As he pulled away, she wanted to hang on to him, never let him go. "I'll go with you."

He held up his hand. "No, you stay with Luna." Running his hand under her chin. "It'll be okay. Trust me darling."

And trust him she did. Standing at the window, she watched the two men get into the beat-up Jeep.

Jane, Galen's wife, came up behind her. "They'll be all right."

Rayn nodded. She held on to those words for the next three hours. That is when Galen, dirty, bruised and bleeding, returned alone.

Rayn knew the worst had happened. She sat silently as Galen told his wife what had happened. When the words... "Heath is dead"...did she pay attention.

Her world crashed. There were a million questions she needed answers for, but the one that demanded its answer first. "Where is his body?"

Galen's lips pressed into a thin line. "He's in the barn. Some of the guys came and helped me get him here."

"...And the couple?" Rayn fought to keep her voice strong.

Galen shook his head. "They were killed too."

Rayn rose to her feet. "So this was all for nothing."

Galen had no answer.

Straightening her back she walked toward the door. "I want to see my husband..." She jerked the door open. "I want to see Heath."

***

Rayn heard footsteps coming up the stairs, across the hall, opening the door. She knew by the sound who it was.

Dray.

His presence filled the room even without her turning around. The click of a closing door, his strides crossing the room.

His arms encircled her. "We'll find them."

Leaning back against him, she relaxed the stiffness. "I know."

They stood in silence. Rayn took in the scent of him. With one motion, she twisted around, backing him up.

A sudden angry strength caused her to push him down on the bed. Straddling him, she clenched her thighs to hold him still. He frowned, then relaxed. Letting his arms lay at his side, he didn't struggle. Rayn allowed the fierce energy of her rage to engulf her. With fervent fingers, she ripped his shirt from his chest. Her fingernails clawed at his skin, leaving a thin line of blood. Bending down to lick the salty liquid, she ran her hands in to his jeans. His manhood hardening as she kneaded it. He started to rise up. She stopped him with more pressure from her legs, one hand shoving him back down.

Rayn need to be in control. It was the beast of her emotions. Dray narrowed his eyes as she took domination over his body. Her hands clasped and massaged him. He closed his eyes as the hardness grew. Looking down on him, she needed to own him, claim him as hers.

Roughly, she pulled him free, releasing her grip just long enough to push his jeans away. Urging his body to feel the climatic release of lust, she induced more pressure. Running her tongue down his passion trail, she felt his trembling.

Rising up on her knees, she impaled herself on his rod. He growled, his body jerked as she rose up and down. His hands reached for her, but she caught them in mid-air, pressed them back down on the bed.

Her body received her own orgasm with a compelling spike. It allowed her to release the deep emotions she had kept bottled. Closing her eyes, she accepted the waves crashing over her, the liberating of her soul. As she slumped down on Dray's body. He slipped from her. His arms caught her as she let go of both her physical and emotional bonds. Their sweat mingled together as he gently laid her next to him. She felt his fingers brushing back the wet hair from her face.

Spent from all the battles in her spirit, she lay still, her eyes closed. The cool breeze from the open window refreshed her hot, sticky body.

Then the tears came. In a flood of unshackled resolve, her determination returned. She turned away from Dray, curled into a ball and sobbed. He permitted her that privilege.

***

Dray paced around the back of the burned-out barn. Carrying one of the powerful guns from the followers' collection, he stood ready to overtake anyone presenting themselves as a threat. This was old hat to him. He had been taught to be on guard all his life. No fear or dread, just a job to be done.

He had borne the honesty of Rayn's anger, was surprised it radiated to him. For once, he felt he was protecting something worthwhile. Never had he considered what he was protecting. He just obeyed the commands to protect. Now it was personal. It was the woman he loved, but also the people she loved and the crusade she believed in. He didn't quite understand why, but after the episode at the rock, the tattoo, the change in his heart and most important of all, the trust of these people, he quit thinking about it. It was what he needed to do. And if some son-of-a-bitch wanted to challenge him...

Bring it on!!

He jerked when he heard a twig snap. Positioning his gun, he saw a figure move in the moonlight. The cocking of his gun made the person stop.

"Dray?" The voice was of one of the men of the house. "Yeah."

The man put his hands up. "It's starting to get daylight. We want to get started on rebuilding the barn."

Dray's suspicions jumped up. "We?"

"The other men." The shadowy figure pointed over his shoulder. "The lumber should be arriving here soon."

Dray still hadn't lowered his gun. "Lumber? Where the hell do you get lumber in the middle of the night?"

The man shrugged. "We have our ways."

Dray chuckled to himself.

No wonder I couldn't catch Rayn at anything. This is a tightly woven network of serious people.

Dray suddenly realized he was still pointing a gun at the man and the man still had his hands in the air. Lowering his gun, Dray spoke firmly. "Put your arms down, come over here so I can see your face.

As the man followed the directions, Dray recognized him. Didn't know his name, but had seen him around. A young man with a family. In all seriousness, he probably could build a barn.

As the man approached, Dray watched his body language. This was not the traitor. This man was here to keep his family together.

"Why the hurry on rebuilding the barn." Dray wanted to know why the rush.

"We figured the quicker we got it rebuilt, the easier it will be to cover-up the fire.

Nice thinking

The man continued. "We figure the Cartel will be here soon, thinking we will be sitting here with half a barn and they can bluff us into telling them Rayn is here." The man stood straighter. "But we will never tell."

His loyalty touched Dray. While Dray had been loyal to the Cartel, it was out of duty, not feelings. But the Insurgents cared for one another. This was a strange phenomenon for Dray. While he loved Rayn more than life itself, which never happened before, caring for the well-being of others had never been his concern.

Now, all of a sudden, he understood. And could even feel it creep into his spirit.

Spirit! Didn't even know I had one!

But, since the rock, he had feelings overtake him so he stopped fighting them. They were a real part of him.

Dray dislodged his gun, put his hand on the man's shoulder. "You're a good man."

The first light of dawn rose over the compounded. Dray looked around. Several men were unloading the lumber. Others were removing the burned debris. Women too helped. He was so engrossed in the activity around him, he didn't heard Galen approach.

Galen's voice made him jerk around. "We made it through the night." He slapped Dray on the shoulder. "Go get a shower and some food. We meet in an hour." Galen glanced sideways at the people around him. No one was paying attention.

84

Dray nodded, started to leave, but turned back. He addressed Galen. "I feel you trust me..." Galen nodded. Dray cocked his head. "...why?"

Galen smiled. "I knew your parents."

Dray was shocked.

Why would my parents know an Insurgent?

"How? Why...?" Dray wanted answers.

Galen shook his head. "Later. We will discuss it later. Not now..." Galen gently pushed Dray. "Go, get cleaned up. We have a lot to do."

Dray walked away, but his head was spinning.

What connection did this have to do with his parents?

Approaching the house, he looked up, saw Rayn standing on the deck waiting for him. Dragging his sleep-weary body up the stairs, he drew her into his empty arms. Kissing her, she smelled like a fresh breeze.

Laughing, she took the gun from him. "Go shower. You still smell like smoke."

He nuzzled her neck. "And you smell really good."

***

Dray followed the group though the command room to a hidden door on the side. Entering a sterile white space, with wall to wall machines. The command post at the Cartel wasn't even close to being this well-equipped.

A table sat in the middle of the room. Each member took a seat. Dray pulled a chair out, sat next to Rayn and Galen.

Rayn addressed the group. "What do we have?"

Seth shook his head. No one else spoke.

Dray spoke up. "Tell me about your staff Seth."

Seth looked up. "Edward came one day, on his own. Angie came with Galen..."

Dray frowned, turning to Galen. "Do you trust her?"

Galen nodded. "She's the daughter of a good friend."

Dray looked around the room at the others. "So, Edward...we need to set a trap for him."

Rayn had remained quiet. Dray could see the anger rising in her. But she wasn't some fragile female that needed to be protected. She was as strong a fighter he had ever seen. No, it was the betrayal that enraged her.

Trust! The whole essence of the mission.

Seth cleared his throat. "I can do that. I know how to make the computers work for me."

Dray looked around at the computers surrounding him. "You do all this?"

Seth grinned. "Yeah, it took a while, but as soon as we got the parts, it was easy."

Dray frowned. "How did you get the parts?"

Seth raised his head, looking at Dray. "We have our ways."

Shrugging, Dray nodded. "Of course you do."

Rayn stood. "So our first course is to trap the traitor, Edward if it is." Her eyes were red from lack of sleep. Her shoulders slumped wearily. "Let's do it. But first, we need to get some sleep."

Galen nodded. "We need to keep watch again tonight or until we know it's safe."

With that the group stood together. Dray followed Rayn out. He stopped for a moment in the first command room.

You'd think this was all they needed.

When the secret door was tightly closed, everything looked back to normal.

Go time.

His fortitude kicked in. To pursue an enemy was his best tactic. He turned to Seth. "Be careful, but work quickly. This person is dangerous."

Seth looked up at him. "So you think it's Edward?"

Dray shook his head. "Don't know, but if it's not, we need to eliminate him fast and look for the real traitor."

Seth turned back to his computer. "Done deal."

Dray patted him on the back.

Taking the steps two at a time, Dray reached their bedroom. Rayn was standing at the window. Walking up behind her, he saw her field of vision was the barn.

Speaking low, he wanted to reassure her. "We'll find the person."

She nodded. "I know. It's just..."

"The betrayal, I get it." He saw her strained smile. "Rayn, I promise..."

She turned to face him, putting her finger to his lips. "I know. I trust you to do this." Walking around him, she went to the bed, sat down. Hanging her head, she took a deep breath. "Let's get some sleep."

***

Rayn stood at the window, the moon cast an eerie glow over the yard. Her mind went back to when her husband first brought her here.

Rayn stepped out of the small, fuel-efficient car. Looking over the house in front of her, she saw a place in the state of total disarray. To her right stood a barn, no make that half a barn. The land stretched for miles with not another house in sight.

"Hon, what is this?" Heath had not told her where they were going when they left their high-rise condo in the City.

Her husband spread out his arms. "I want to live here."

"Why?"

She watched the muscles in his back tense as he talked. "Life as we know it is going to end." He turned toward her. "Not tomorrow, maybe not even for years, but we need to make ourselves self-sufficient. The economy will not be able to stand much longer."

Rayn had seen the signs also. She and Heath shared the same profession, finance. Walking up behind Heath, she wrapped her arms around his waist, laid her head on his back. She trusted him, trusted his instincts.

Rayn spoke softly. "So, we become farmer and farmette Jones?" She wanted to keep the tone light. Watching her husband these last months, carrying what seemed like the weight of the world on his shoulders, she allowed him to work it out.

The muscles in his back vibrated, letting her know he was chuckling. "Something like that."

"Okay..." She stepped away from him. "How is this going to go down?"

The sound of another car on the gravel road made both of them turn. Rayn smiled to herself.

Galen and Jane, their two best friends, bounced in the small car as it came to a halt next to the couple.

Heath slipped his hand into Rayn's. "Welcome folks..." He waved his free hand. "...to our piece of paradise."

Galen walked around his car. Nodding his head. "Nice."

Rayn narrowed her eyes. "You knew about this?"

"Yeah, we have talked about it for a while."

Rayn looked over at Jane. "You?"

Jane nodded.

Rayn looked from face to face. "So why was I kept out of the loop?"

Heath rubbed her still flat belly. "When you told me you were pregnant, I knew we had to engage the plan."

Rayn placed her hand over Heath's. "So, tell me how this will work?"

Heath encircled her shoulders, pulled her to him. "Well, the land is bought..."

Rayn pulled back to look at him.

He shrugged. "...it just came together. Galen and I will get the house livable. Little by little we will move in."

Rayn pinched her brows. "We? We are all going to live together?"

The men grinned.

Jane walked over to Rayn. "At first. We need to get a lot done in a short amount of time. Plus..." Jane's eyes went to Rayn's belly. "...I need to be here to help you give birth."

Rayn's eyes got big. Jane was a doctor and would be the one to deliver her baby...but... "You guys seemed to have this already planned."

Heath stepped away. "Sorry babe, but we need to get started."

Galen shuffled over to Heath. "We just wanted to take care of you Rayn."

Rayn could feel the love from these dear people and Heath, her husband. Nodding, she surrendered. "Okay. Tell me what to do."

The three smiled together. For the first time in months, she saw relief on Heath's face. He must have felt so much pressure trying to get things done while worrying about her and their child.

The men took off over the field, pointing and talking. Jane took hold of Rayn's arm. Together they walked toward the house that would be their next home.

Jane squeezed Rayn's arm. "It will all work out."

Rayn had faith in her words, the same faith she had for this dear friend. Walking up the steep steps, a board broke under her foot.

This will be quite the undertaking.

Rubbing her belly.

But we will keep you safe my child. I promise.

***

Trust.

Rayn pushed her hair out of her eyes. This farm, this life, all of this had been built on trust.

Now some fool had gone and screwed that up!

So absorbed in her thoughts, she had not heard Dray come up behind her. His body barely touched hers, but she could feel the warmth from his skin.

"Sorry, didn't mean to wake you." Keeping her back to him.

His voice washed over her. "You were having some deep thoughts. It was hard to stay asleep with so much activity going on. Care to share?"

Rayn bowed her head.

He deserved to know.

"I was thinking back to when the farm first become a reality." She leaned forward, placing both hands on the window frame.

"Tell me about it." Dray's voice was away from her.

She turned to see he had taken a seat in a chair across the room. Looking into his patient eyes, she leaned against the ledge, both hands on the wood. "We came when I first knew I was pregnant."

"We?" Dray leaned back, all his attention on her.

"My husband, Heath, Galen and his wife Jane..."

"You never speak of your husband."

Rayn felt a sadness come over her. "It's painful."

He nodded his understanding. "And Jane?"

"Galen's wife died of cancer, about two years before everything changed."

"Tell me how it changed, Rayn. What made you become such a Insurgent?"

Rayn walked over to the stool in front of Dray. Sitting down she looked at her hands. "Luna was about five when the monetary structure of the country failed. Any money in the banks were gone. Any cash on hand was worthless. People lost homes, jobs and then..." Saying the words cut through her heart. "...they took away the children."

Dray frowned as if he remembered it.

Rayn narrowed her eyes. "How old were you when it changed?"

"Fifteen, I think. My father was in the military. One day he came home, said I was to join the Cartel. I didn't mind, never asked why. Just did as I was told."

"Of course you did. If the teenagers would join the Cartel, they wouldn't be sent to the camps."

A look of surprise crossed his eyes. "I never thought about the children...I picked some up once, they were crying, their parents were screaming. I just did my duty." His eyes begged forgiveness. "I'm sorry..."

Rayn patted his hand. "We did what we had to do." She stood, pulling him up with her. "Don't beat yourself up."

Dray drew her into him. "I wish I had known you before all this happened."

Rayn hit him jokingly on the chest. "You were fifteen! I was a wife and mother. You wouldn't have even noticed me."

"Oh I would have noticed..." A wicked smile play around his lips. "...I would have like to have seen you barefoot and pregnant."

Rayn shook her head. "You are despicable."

"Maybe." He nuzzled her neck.

Why do I love this man? We are worlds apart, but I feel him in my soul.

CHAPTER TEN

The hot midday sun beat down on Dray's bare back. Pounding the nail into the plank, he was amazed at the speed in which the barn rose from the ashes. The people of the farm made it look exactly like the original structure. Weathered and old, no one could tell it was just built.

So involved with his task, Dray had not heard the approaching person. Her soft voice washed over him like a mist. "Dray."

The familiar voice sounded out of place, it came from another time and place. Lowering his hammer, he turned to see a ghost of his past before him. The young girl stood a ways from him, the daylight danced on her honey colored hair. His eyes traveled to her swollen belly, heavy with a baby.

Dray laid his hammer on the worktable, unable to move, he searched her face. "Tesla?"

Rubbing her hand over her round stomach, she smiled shyly. "Yeah, it's me."

Tesla was one of his former lovers. A sweet girl he had sex with, never expecting to see again until the urge returned and he needed a release.

Spreading his arms out, he had a million questions, but one topped the list. He did the math in his head. It had been several months since he had seen her. Memories of the last time washed over him. It was one of the days he had come to the farm, after one of the many battles with Ryan.

He would return to the camp highly charged and sexually aroused. Wanting Ryan to be the woman to satisfy him, he would instead turn to the first available woman back at the Fort. The last time it had been Tesla.

That would have been seven or eight months ago.

Tesla smiled up at him. "Yes, she's yours."

He released the breath he didn't realize he had been holding. "She?"

Tesla nodded. "It's a girl."

Suddenly, the sun seemed very hot. He looked around. There was a wooden bench under a large shade tree. Taking Tesla's elbow, he guided her to the place she could sit down. Awkwardly she flopped down. Dray put his foot up on the bench, leaned in on his raised knee.

Frowning, he was having a hard time getting all this in his head. "How? Why are you here?"

Tesla folded her hands across her belly. "It was strange. When I found out I was pregnant, I didn't want it taken from me. It changed my whole perspective of life and love..." Her eyes softened. "...I just knew I couldn't stay in the compound. And..." a saddness crossed her eyes. "...I didn't believe you would help me so..."

Dray felt her pain. The emotion surprised him.

I wouldn't have banked on me either.

"...I found the underground to the Insurgents. My parents helped me." Finishing her explanation, she took a deep breath, leaned back, the heavy weight of the child forcing her to shift her position.

Dray lowered his foot. Stood straight, accepting what he had just been told.

A child. A girl. His daughter.

The impacted almost knocked him off his feet. Instead, he sat down next to Tesla. He believed her that it was his. Remembering his time with her, she was always truthful and accepting.

He picked up her hand. "Are you feeling okay?"

She chuckled. "As well as I can."

"Is there a doctor to take care of you?"

"Yes, the doctor here is great." She smiled at his concern.

"What are your plans?"

Tesla raised her head to the sky. "To raise my...our daughter in a place where she is free."

Dray pressed his lips together. "Can I be part of that..." He reached out his hand slowly and touched her belly. "...of her?"

94

Tesla looked over at him. "Yes. Now you can."

He cocked his head. "You say that with such certainty now. What changed?"

Running her hand over his cheek, she smiled at him. "You did. I have watched you since you got here. You believe in the Cause now."

"Yeah, I do. And..."

Should I tell her I love Rayn?

Her voice cut through his thoughts. "And you are finally able to be with the woman you love."

Her words startled him. "I'm sorry...?"

She placed her finger on his lips. "It's okay. I always knew you loved someone else." She chuckled. "I just never suspected it was the head of the Insurgents."

Dray shook his head. "It was something I tried to fight." He looked at her with all honesty. "But I can't deny it anymore."

"It's okay. We understand."

Dray frowned. "We?"

"Your daughter and I. Know that she was conceived in love." Tesla smiled. "I loved...no still do, love you."

Her words were a comfort and a spike to his heart. "Anything you need, let me know."

"We will."

At that moment something bumped the hand he had rested on her stomach. He looked down, laughed. "What was that?"

"Your daughter is telling you she is glad to meet you."

The whole thing became real to Dray. He was a father. And the world changed. He had a reason to fight the Cartel. He knew in his heart of hearts he would never let them take her from him.

And a voice whispered in his ear like a breeze.

Now you are getting it.

***

Ryan stood at the head of the dining table. She had called a meeting of the leaders to plan a strategy. They had a traitor. They needed to be looking for anything irregular. Looking around the table at Galen, Luna, Archer and Dray, her eyes went to the others she had invited Seth, Casper, the foreman of the farm and Piper, who ran the house.

These were people she relied on. She prayed her trust was not misplaced. Taking in a deep breath, she stood straight and strong. "Folks, it can be no secret that we have an enemy among us."

Piper and Casper looked at each other. Casper spoke. "We figured as much. The barn burning pretty much clinched it."

Rayn directed her attention to the couple. "Any idea who?"

Both shook their heads. Casper continued. "We have tried to figure it out, but no, we have nothing." He looked around the group. "Any of you?"

Rayn spoke for the group. "No, us either." She placed both hands on the table, studying the grains of wood. "But this much I know, we will find them. Keep an eye open. Report anything usual, or that raises your suspicions."

Confident she had their support, she raised up her eyes. "Now we need a plan." She turned to Galen.

Galen held up his phone. "Seth has downloaded everyone's history. Why they came here, when they came here, where they came from. Scan them, see if anything doesn't ring true."

Everyone nodded. Galen handed each one a device. Only a few devices existed at the farm. These could be traced only by Seth.

Galen spoke harshly. "We need to keep our suspicions quiet. Talk about it only amongst yourselves and be careful who is around you."

Dray picked up his device, tucked it in his pocket, nodded at Rayn.

Rayn gave him a wry smile. "Okay folks. Do your homework. Do it well."

Everyone left in different directions. Dray walked over to Rayn. She wanted to just throw herself into his arms, make all this go away.

"It's not going to happen that way." His words made her smile.

She looked into the steel gray eyes. "I know but I wish it would."

He draped his arm over her shoulders. "Let's walk. We need to talk."

Rayn knew what was coming. She at known about Tesla since the first day she arrived. It took the young girl awhile before she admitted who the father was. At first, Rayn was outraged. She wanted to strangle Dray. But now things were different, she wanted to know his thoughts.

Allowing him to lead her, they walked a path by the stream. He was quiet, she allowed him his space.

At the water's edge, he picked up a stone, tossing it across the water. It skipped three times.

Without looking at her, he started to speak. "I just found out...there is a girl at the farm..." He paused. She waited. He continued. "I guess I am going to be a father."

Rayn smiled to herself. "You guess? I think that is a definite yes or no."

He turned to look back at her. "You're right. I am going to be a father." She could barely hear his words. "A daughter."

"And how does that make you feel."

He ran his hand through his hair. "Wow. All sorts of things. Surprised, pleased, scared..." He shook his head. "...protective." He drew her to him. "I know I will do whatever it takes to keep her safe." He frowned at her. "How does that make you feel?"

Rayn put her arms around his neck. "I am happy for you. This must have been the plan for you. Now you know how I...we all feel."

"I do. And I know now why I am here." He pulled back to look at her. "But, you know, I love you. Tesla was a means to an end. I care for her, will be there for the birth and raising of our daughter." He frowned, waiting for her to respond.

"I know. I am good with it. We love on a different level. And there are many kinds of love. Enjoying loving your daughter." She stood on her tip-toes, took his lips in a sweet, but passionate kiss. He groaned, picked her up.

Lost in their own world, they were interrupted by Galen. "The troops are coming. We need to hide you two."

The three of them ran to the middle of the field, raising the grass covered door, Rayn and Dray moved down the stairs, while Galen shut the door behind them.

***

The low roar of the cycles vibrated the deck as Luna and Archer waited for their arrival. Several of the other house members stood behind them. Other members were stationed around the area.

Bono led the troops. Sitting proud and cocky, his eyes were hid by his dark sunglasses. Luna knew too well the hateful look behind them. Gripping Archer's hand tightly, she wanted to display a strong presence to match her mother's. Raising her chin, she planted her feet on the platform.

Bono stopped a few feet from the steps. Lifting his glasses to rest on his head, he balanced the cycle with both feet on the ground. Removing his gloves, slow, deliberate, he stared at the young couple. Dismounting, he walked toward the house. Luna and Archer met him at the bottom of the stairs.

Squinting his eyes, Bono looked over at the barn. "I heard you had a fire?" He turned back. "But the barn looks well intact."

Archer gave Bono a smug smile. "Why do you ask only about the barn?"

Bono narrowed his eyes into a sharp look. "I just assumed…"

Luna spoke up. "I guess you assumed wrong. The barn is fine, as are all the rest of the buildings." Crossing her arms, she spoke with confidence. "You must have been misinformed."

Bono let a strong silence hang between them. Luna held her words. Finally, Bono spoke. "Mind if we take a look at it."

Luna shrugged. "Knock yourself out." As Bono turned, motioning to his men, Luna stepped down to the solid ground. "You don't mind if we tag along. You know, just to keep everything on the up and up?"

Bono grunted. "Suit yourself." His men had left their bikes, some scattered around the yard, into the house. Five men walked with Bono, like a human shield.

Archer and Luna followed the entourage.

At the door, Galen greeted the group. "Welcome General Bono. What brings you to our fair abode?"

Bono glared at him. "Cut the crap. You had a fire, the barn burned to the ground..."

Galen stepped back. "And you know this how?"

"I saw it, you idiot. From the bluff." Bono pushed open one of the horse's stalls. Two of his men followed him. The other three went to different areas in the barn.

Galen took a stand by Luna and Archer. "You must have been looking in the wrong direction..."

Bono jerked around sharply, glaring at Galen.

Galen spoke with an accent of heavy sarcasm. "Sir."

Bono stepped back into the passageway. His other men joined him, shaking their heads.

Archer took Luna's hand.

Bono glared at all three of them. "You did a good job of recovering from the fire. I applaud your craftsmanship." He looked up and around the structure, then down at them.

The three didn't answer him. Bono scowled at them, then brushed past.

At the door he turned, walked back to the three. Focusing his attention on Luna, his tone was harsh and threatening. "And, young lady, you are a cheap imitation of your mother." He chuckled as vile words came out of his mouth. "Speaking of Rayn, I don't suppose you have heard from her?"

Luna took a deep breath. Her mother taught her well. *Stay in control. Don't let them see you sweat.*

"No, General Bono. I do not know where my mother is." She raised an eye brow. "Do you?"

That disturbed his resolve. "I will find her and my lieutenant, never you fear."

Luna cocked her head. "You, General Bono, I do not fear"

General Bono's face turned bright red. "Listen bitch..." Archer and Galen stepped up to Luna's side. Bono looked at them, then stepped back. "I will take you and all your "people" down." His frustration showed in his words and actions. He shook a finger at Luna.

Luna gave him a strong look. "Like I say, knock yourself out. General Bono."

He turned on his heels, stomped out the barn door, followed by his faithful men.

Galen, Archer and Luna walked to the large opening, watched as all the little men obeyed Bono's quick commands, filtering out of the yard in precise formation.

Luna felt familiar hands on her shoulders, her mother's voice. "You did good daughter."

Luna leaned back against the welcome body of Rayn. "How do you stand that man? I just want to...knock the shit out of him."

Rayn chuckled. "Been there, wanted to. You just have to keep calm. He's not worth it."

Dray walked around to face Luna. "You did good kid." He put his thumb up.

Luna pulled away from Rayn, her fear must have shown on her face. "Dray. He really wants to kill you. Even more than Mom. I saw it in his eyes."

Dray chucked her chin. "I know, darling. But I'm smarter than him."

Luna took in Dray's strong smile. Rayn's voice echoed in her ear. "That doesn't take much."

***

"How did you know when to raid the farm?" Rayn asked the question he had dreaded from the first moment he pulled her from the dark cell.

Dray tried to avoid her eyes, then sighed, looking at her dead on. "We had an informant in the farm."

"Who?" Rayn's eyes blaze fire.

Dray knew he was on soft ground here. It could shift either way. "I don't know. We referred to him as The Farmer."

"Catchy name." Rayn smirked. "Why didn't you tell me before?"

"I was trying to find him before you knew of him." Dray watched her expression. It was hard, unemotional, almost cruel.

Rayn broke the stare down with a blink. "Can you find him?"

"I think so. But I don't know if it is a him or her. No name was ever said." He knew betrayal was the worse crime to Rayn.

Her sigh was one of a heavy burden. "Then let's find him slash *her.*"

"Seth and I are working on it." Dray let go of the breath he was holding.

Rayn relaxed her stance. "Tell me what you know."

Dray took on his get-down-to-business tone. "The person..." He grinned. "...has access to a computer. The messages came over the Net."

Rayn narrowed her eyes. "That means it's either Seth, Angie or Edward."

Dray grimaced. "Not necessary. I am sure there are several people here with tech knowledge."

"Well, that is like a needle in a haystack."

Dray smiled. "There's a lot of hay around here."

Rayn couldn't help but smile.

Dray took hold of her hands. "No pun intended." Drawing her into his arms, he caressed her back. "Come here. It will work itself out."

Rayn melted into his body. "You do know you are bad for my concentration."

Kissing her neck, his mouth lingered over her lips. "Good. You are way too serious."

With a gentle punch to his stomach, she spoke against his mouth. "You are so bad."

His mouth covered hers in a deep, probing kiss. Rayn responded with the fire of her purpose and the flames of her conviction.

"So how will you find him..." Rayn smiled, angling her head. "...her?"

Dray took her hand started walking toward the house. "I am meeting with Seth. We are going to come up with a plan...to catch..." He stopped, turned to Rayn. "...them."

"So, you think there are more than one."

"I really can't tell at this point."

Rayn patted his chest. "Go find them." She turned in the opposite direction. "I need to take care of some things."

Dray stood still as he watched her walk away. He wanted to ask where, what...but kept his thoughts to himself. Turning toward the house he figured going to meet with Seth was the best idea for now.

***

Dray looked over Seth's shoulder as his fingers moved over the computer screen, bring up image after image. The face of the small screen was transferred to the larger screen on the wall.

102

Seth talked as he worked. "No new transmissions have been sent. I guess blocking them stopped the traitor for a while. However..." He enlarge one image. "...they are trying to reach their contact."

Dray straightened up, studying the large screen. "How do you know?"

Seth's curser pointed to a small icon in the corner. "See that?"

Squinting, Dray saw the small green circle. "Yeah?"

"It's the Cartel's mark. It is searching for a certain computer."

"Why can't it find it?"

"Because the computer it wants is shut off."

Dray looked at the black screens of the several computers in the room. "Why do you shut them off?"

"For the very reason it is searching. So it can't find its target."

The little green icon disappeared. Dray studied the large screen. "It's gone! Where did it go?"

Seth chuckled. "It only searches for a few seconds at a time. It doesn't want to get caught."

Dray placed his hands on his hips. "Let's catch it."

Seth pursed his lips. "Okay..." His fingers worked over the keys again. "...go turn on all the computers."

Dray nodded, went around the room flipping the switches. Returning back to Seth, he watched the green icon reappear.

"Game on!" The excitement in Seth's voice could not be contained. He stood up, scanning the room for the one computer it would connect with. "Bingo!" His look located a computer in the far corner of the room.

Dray followed his gaze. "Whose computer is that?"

"No one's. That's why we had to search for the line to us. It's an unused computer, so to speak."

Dray walked over to the renegade machine. There was nothing to tell who had used it, if ever. "Shut this one off. Put a key logger on it, then keep it on, but not so anyone notices."

"Good call. I'll get that done." Seth worked his keyboard like a pianist at Carnegie Hall.

Dray paced around the room. A plan was forming in his head.

Soon they would have their traitor.

Seth's high pitched voice broke Dray's train of thought. "Done. Now what sir?"

Dray smiled at the word 'sir'. Even though they had accepted him, they still remembered where he came from.

Walking back over to Seth, he patted the young geek's shoulders. "Now we wait."

***

Rayn didn't have any place to be, she just needed to get away alone for a while, to clear her mind, feed her soul.

Going to a tall weeping willow at the corner of the first pasture, she sat down on the rocks under it. Putting her hands on her knees, she bowed her head.

Guide me

You are not lost. You are going through shifts and changes, but the direction is still the same. Have the courage to know your soul is leading.

The words brought comfort to her. She believed in the leader of the pack, so to speak.

Thank you.

Her spirit rose up strong and ready for the fight. But, for these few minutes, she needed to be still.

CHAPTER ELEVEN

General Bono stomped down the hall of the office complex. His red face and heavy breathing were definite signs of a rage about to explode.

Lieutenant Milo dismissed the men, followed Bono into the general's office.

Bono threw his helmet across the room, with one sweep of his arm cleared his desk. "That young bitch is as bad as her mom."

Milo stood in front of the desk. There was no good reason to respond to the general's outburst, so he stayed quiet, his hands behind his back.

Bono ranted on. "How did they rebuild that barn so fast?" He ran his hand over his bald head. "It looked like it had been standing there for centuries." Fixing his steel gaze on the young officer, he roared. "Say something!"

Milo looked Bono in the eyes. "What's to say, Sir? They are a clever and creative group."

Bono plopped down on his chair. "Damn! Damn! I will break them." He pounded his fist on the desktop. "And where the hell is Dray?"

Milo shook his head. "I have no idea, Sir. I suspect he is at the farm with Rayn, but we can't find them."

"And our informant?" Bono stared at the young officer. "Where is he?"

"He's there. They have blocked his transmissions to us. We are trying to communicate with him now."

Bono leaned forward. "And how is that working out for us?"

Milo grimaced. "Not so good yet, but I will go check on the progress."

"You do that." Bono leaned back in his chair. "Then let me know where we stand."

Milo bowed. "Yes sir." He turned on his heels. He was glad to have been sent away to do something other than watch a grown man throw a childish fit.

The computer center was housed in an underground shelter across the compound. The bright sun hit Milo's eyes in a blinding light. Putting on his sunglasses, he walked to a plain, square building. Entering the darkness, he needed to remove the glasses. Swiping his card on the first door, it slid open revealing a long walkway. Following the yellow line down the middle, at the end, he turned right. Another door greeted him. Again swiping his card, when it opened, a set of stairs descended before him. Low incandesce lamps lit the way. At the bottom, he again swiped, this door opened into a large room full of computers and people.

The military always had the newest and best technology. How the Insurgents had out smarted them always confused Milo.

What did they possess that could skirt around the Cartel as well as they had?

The room went quiet when he entered. Everyone stopped what they were doing to stare at the intruder.

A middle-aged man in a white coat stood. "Lieutenant Milo?"

Milo nodded to the man. "Dexter. I am here to check on the transmissions from The Farmer."

Dexter smiled. "We have good news. We found an open computer. I was just sending an encrypted message to him."

Milo looked at the words on the screen. "And you are sure the Insurgents don't suspect a thing?"

"Of course not." Dexter laughed. "They aren't that smart or well equipped." Dexter puffed out his chest. "We have the best of the best and the most advanced technology available."

Milo raised an eyebrow. "Don't underestimate them."

Dexter sat back down. His fingers flying over the screen. A simple message: Contact the command center. Snapping the send icon, the words disappeared. "It's on its way."

Milo stood with his arms crossed, watching the screen.
Nothing

Looking up at the rest of the room, several of people looked away from him. It was a room full of the best techno minds on the planet. Both men and women, they spend their days controlling the world through machines.

Then why can't we crack through the Insurgents firewalls?

A dinging sound drew his attention back to Dexter's computer.

I am here

"See, there it is!!" Dexter's excitement was huge. "What do you want me to tell him?"

Milo narrowed his eyes. Something seemed wrong. He couldn't put his finger on what. "Ask him if Dray and Rayn are at the farm."

Dexter touched the keyboard on the screen. When he hit send, he leaned back.

Soon one word came back. "Yes."

Dexter looked up at Milo. "What do you want me to say?"

Milo bent down, checked out the screen. Everything looked fine. "Tell him 'good work'. And to stay in touch."

Dexter did as he was told. The message went over invisible wires back to the farm.

Milo took another look around the room. His eye caught a young girl watching him. For some reason she struck a chord of concern. When she saw he was looking at her, she quickly turned away.

Keeping his eyes on her, he spoke to Dexter. "Send me all the transmissions from The Farmer. I'll let you know how to respond."

Dexter nodded. "Very good sir. So, we found the renegade couple."

Milo had a strange feeling in his gut. "Don't count on it. Just keep the line to The Farmer open." As he spoke the name, he noticed that the young girl looked over at him.

He needed to find out more about their spy.

Leaving the isolated room, Milo stopped outside before going to his office. Leaning against the concrete wall of the one of the buildings, his mind flashed back to memories of when he and Dray first came to the compound.

***

"Milo, get the one on your right, dude." Dray's voice carried the commanding tone that would serve him well later in life.

Milo blasted the icon with his laser. The boys were playing a video game in Dray's house. Growing up together in military families, living in the standard provided housing, the boys had always known each other.

"Good shot." Dray let his excitement soar.

Both so involved in the game they had not heard Dray's father enter.

"Boys..." The commanding voice made them both drop their attack. "...we need to talk."

Dray stood. "What's going on Sir?"

Captain Silo Konner's, Dray's father, face carried a pinched look. "Things are getting ready for a change." He sighed deeply. "You boys need to join the forces of the Cartel."

Milo stood next to his friend. Both nodded.

Silo's face broke into a look of pride. "Good. You report tomorrow morning to General Bono at the military compound in the Fort." In a stifled motion, he started to reach out to his son, but pulled back. "You are good boys. You will serve..." His voice cracked. "...well." He turned sharply, walked out of the room.

Dray looked over at Milo. "I guess game time is over. We are now going to do the real thing."

Milo nodded.

***

Milo's dad was a rough, heavy-drinking man, who had no use for his family. They were a means to his advancement. Nothing more.

Growing up, Milo learned quickly to stay out of the man's way, so most of his time was spent either with Dray or studying at the school. Milo had a mind like a steel trap. Everything stayed there until he called it up. But it was logic that served him best. His intuition was point on. He could dissect a situation quickly and thoroughly.

So, when they were called up to join the Cartel, he knew it was where he was meant to be. One thing, Milo had a kindness in him that came from too many harsh words and blunt force actions. He could charm anyone into telling him what he wanted to know.

Unlike Dray, who was just charming in an alpha male way, Milo could get under the surface. It didn't surprise Milo that Dray moved up the ranks quicker, or was the popular choice to be General Bono's right hand.

They both believed in the Cartel until...

How did the Insurgent woman get Dray to change his alliance?

Milo finished the walk to his office. Not passing anyone, he walked briskly down the hall.

Going to his desk, he booted up his computer. As promised, Dexter sent all the transmissions from The Farmer. Sitting down, he scrolled through them. His mind sorting as he went. Something at the edge of the words nagged at him. The Farmer's correspondence had be silence for several days. Now it came unchallenged.

Why now?

Milo had never heard of The Farmer until Dray left. Then, all of sudden, they had a spy in the Insurgent camp.

Did Dray know about The Farmer?

Lord help the spy, any spy that was caught by Dray.

Milo had observed Dray's cunning abilities to smoke out fake people.

A thought tugged at the back of Milo's mind.

What if Dray was setting a trap? If so, our spy just walked into it.

***

Dray leaned back in the chair. He was in a secret room watching a camera set on the tech room. The small, dark room's only light came from the screen. Dray watched the monitor with the Cartel's logo. A shadowy figure moved to the computer. Dray sat up, leaning forward. The lean fingers moved over the keyboard. Dray squinted to read the words. He spread his fingers over the screen to enlarge the writing.

I am here.

Where have you been?

They are suspicious. I needed to lay low. I think they know the code.

Are Dray and Rayn there?

A pause.

Dray held his breath.

The figure's hands hovered over the keyboard. Then it typed the words that would seal its fate.

Yes.

Dray jumped up from his seat. Blasting through the room's door, he traveled down the stairs at a neck-breaking speed. As he rounded the corner, he saw what appeared to be a male figure heading swiftly outside. By the time Dray reached him, they were at the barn. He grabbed the back of the person's shirt, jerking him around. The face revealed the traitor.

Edward.

Dray shoved Edward against the barn wall. "What the fuck do you think you're doing?"

Edward threw his hands in the air. "Sorry man. I had to..."

Consumed with anger, Dray's face burned from the heat of his own rage. "Explain!"

Edward's eyes betrayed his fear. "They have my mother and kid sister..."

Relaxing his hold, Dray allowed Edward to slip down the wall. He knew the means in which the Cartel recruited people. Standing over the man, Dray kneeled down. "Tell me everything." Pointing his finger in Edward's face. "And don't lie. I need the truth or I am going to turn you over the people in the house."

Edward's head bobbed up and down. "We were on our way here when one of the troops caught us. Dragging us in front of Bono, he decided to use me to penetrate the Insurgents since I knew computers. He told me I would never see family again if I didn't do it."

Tears streamed down Edward's face. Dray stood up. He knew too well how the Cartel worked. Edward had every right to believe what they told him.

Placing his hands on his waist, Dray glared down at the sniveling man. "Tell me what you have told them."

Edward crept up the wall. "They want to know if you and Rayn are here."

"And you told them?"

"Well I tried to tell them, but Seth stopped the message."

"And the barn?"

"You were right. It was a smoke screen to get their attention."

"And did it?"

"Yes, that's why they came." Edward shook his head. "But I couldn't get to them."

Dray shrugged.

Good plan people, to rebuild the barn as quickly as they did!

Edward looked at Dray with pleading eyes. "So, what are you going to do now?"

Dray grabbed the collar of Edward's shirt. "We are going to send them another message."

Half hauling half dragging, Dray pulled Edward out of the barn. With a death grip on the man, he hauled him up the deck stairs, shoving him into the house.

Rayn and Galen came running out of the command room, took one look at Edward and understood immediately what was going on. Rayn started for Edward, but Dray grabbed her hand to stop her from slapping Edward. She narrowed her eyes at Dray.

Dray lowered her arm. "He's going to help us."

Rayn jerked her arm away from him. "What makes you think he can be trusted?"

"They have his mother and sister. It was the only way he could keep them safe."

A spark of compassion crossed Rayn's eyes. She looked over at Galen.

Galen bowed his head, a smirk on his face. "Makes sense." He looked up at Dray. "What's your plan?"

"He sends another message saying Rayn and I left to form another safe house. West. We will send them west." Dray snickered.

Looking over at Rayn, Dray waited for her reaction.

Rayn sighed. "Okay, sounds like a good plan. But..." she pointed a finger at Edward. "You screw me over and I'll kill you."

Edward's eyes said he believed her. "Yes ma'am."

The four of them walked to the command room. As they opened the door, Seth and Angie swung around from their computers. Angie's eyes widened with surprise.

Seth frowned, his eyes went from Edward to Dray. "What's going on? Edward?"

Edward shuffled his feet, looked at the ground.

Seth returned his look to Dray. Standing, he addresses the soldier. "Dray?"

Dray scowled. "Edward is our traitor."

Seth walked up to Edward. "Seriously? You betrayed the whole Cause? For what?"

Edward raised his eyes to Seth, but all he did was mummer and shake his head.

"The Cartel has his mother and sister. They forced him to spy on us." Dray spoke with a touch of empathy.

Seth looked over Edward's head, to Rayn and Galen. "So what do we do now?"

Rayn shrugged. "Dray has a plan."

Seth turned his attention back to Dray. "And it is...?"

"We send a message to them with false information. Maybe...just maybe, it will get them off our back for a while."

Seth bit his lower lip. "It worth a try. But..."

"But what?" Dray watched Seth's face.

Seth looked back at Angie, then his computer. "They changed the code to track them. It took me three weeks to crack it before. They must know we are on to them."

Dray jerked sharply toward Edward. "Do they?"

Edward nodded. "Yeah, I told them."

Seth sat down at his screen. "Okay, I'll start working on it."

Dray cocked his head. "I know where the code is." Everyone turned to look at him. "I'll go get it."

Rayn narrowed her eyes. "Just like that. You'll go get it?"

Dray chuckled. "It's not that big of a deal. Things are only protected from the outside. Inside, it is easy to get things."

Rayn put her hands on her hips. "And if you get caught?"

Dray walked pass her, kissing her lightly. "Then it's been nice knowing you all."

Crossing the house with easy steps, Dray bounced up the stairs to the bedroom. Opening his backpack, he removed a plastic card. Turning around he saw Rayn blocking the door. Her look was one of fear. He walked over to her, pulled her into his arms.

"Don't go." Her eyes were forming tears.

He kissed her, drawing her body into him. "I'll be all right. I know what I'm doing."

Pulling back, she searched his face. "Please be careful."

"I will darling. But this is the quickest way."

Releasing him, she stepped back. "Go with the Power."

Dray winked at her. "I will."

Jumping down the stairs, he went outside. There he found Galen mounted on a horse, a spare next to him.

Dray smiled walked over, took the reins. Lifting up onto the leather saddle, he grinned at Galen.

Galen nodded. "We'll ride to the bluff. I'll wait there for you."

Dray turned his horse toward the north. Riding at a gallop, they soon reached the top of the bluff. Dray pulled up his horse.

The township lay out in front of them. All he had to do was scale down the cliff and enter the gated area.

Dismounting, he handed the reins to Galen. "If I'm not back by dusk, get out of here."

"Okay, but I trust you will be successful. The Power be with you."

Dray turned, half walked, half slid down the rocks. Reaching the gate, he slipped his plastic card into the slot.

Praying they had not changed the code on this gate, he held his breath until the lock clicked and the gate opened. Slipping inside quickly, he shut the iron gate before it set off an alarm.

Moving quietly and sure, Dray followed close to the buildings until he found the building he had called his home for most of his adult life. Slipping in the door, he was relieved that the hallway stood empty. Going to his former room, he pulled the door open. It was as he left it, mostly. He could tell someone had searched it. But he had made sure there were no traces of his life outside of the Cartel. Going to his computer, he logged on. The system was set up to detect any outside connections, but he had about five minutes to find the new code. Working the keyboard standing up, he found the access, quickly copied down the new code.

Shutting down the computer, he looked around his old living space. A lot had changed. Instead of the sterile room, where his routine mainly stayed the same, he now woke every morning not know what the day would bring. Sharing it with a woman he loved, not just slept with.

Shaking his head to clear his thoughts, he went to the door and checked the hall. Finding it clear, he slipped out again. As he passed by General Bono's door, he was surprised it stood wide open. He couldn't help himself, he stepped in. Walking over to the large table in the middle of the room, he glanced at the papers spread out. Large maps of the area, with notations of planned attacks. The farm was one. Scheduled for tomorrow.

He heard a door open down the way, voices coming toward him. Slipping behind the main door, he flattened himself against the wall. Through the crack he could see General Bono stop to finish his conversation with Lieutenant Milo.

"We'll go tomorrow. I know Dray and that bitch Rayn are there." Dray winced at the remark about Rayn. "Since we haven't heard from our source, I figure he got caught."

Lieutenant Milo grimaced. "You are probably right, Sir."

"Good, we are on the same page. Brief the men." Bono turned, entered the room, shut the door. Dray stayed in his spot, watching the general walk to his desk and sit down.

It took a few seconds before Bono looked up and saw Dray. "Well, well, well..." Bono leaned back in his chair. "...what have we here? The runaway Lieutenant Draven Konner." A smirk crossed his face. "And where is your muse?"

Dray pushed off from the wall. "Somewhere safe, where you will never find her."

"Don't be so sure. I have my means."

Dray nodded. "I'm sure you do." As he talked, he moved cautiously to the door handle.

Bono, so cocky and full of himself, didn't notice the slight movements. "So have you come crawling back to be the soldier you were meant to be?"

"Not hardly." Dray twisted the knob behind his back. As it turned, he stepped to the side, pulled the door slightly open.

Bono stood up. "So you have joined the Insurgents? Did you find that cause that you so needed?"

Dray stopped his movement. "I wasn't searching for a cause." He frowned at the words. Something clicked in his mind.

Bono is trying to tell me something.

He searched the elder man's face.

Bono crossed his arms over his chest. "Yeah you are. And you will meet an untimely death, just like your parents."

The words slapped Dray across the face. "What do my parents have to do with anything?"

Bono chuckled. "They saw the light, so to speak. Were on their way to join the resistance...well, you know what happened."

A coldness settled over Dray. "You had a hand in that?"

"Of course, couldn't have the parents of my first Lieutenant on the other side.

Dray clenched his fists at his side. Forgetting about his safely, he took long strides, reaching the desk. "You bastard."

Bono leaned into Dray's face. "So give it and her up, or you will find yourself dead in a ditch.

Then it hit Dray.

This man was evil, pure and simple.

Thoughts of Rayn shot through his mind.

Get to her. Forget about Bono for now.

Turning on his heels, Dray bolted from the room. Checking for other people, he ran down the empty hall, hitting the outside door with a bang. At a dead run, he saw the fence looming in front of him. Taking a leap, he hit the wires half way, scrambling over the rest of the way. He could hear the alarm go off behind him, the sounds of running feet, shouts to "Halt!"

Jumping down from the top, he hit the ground in a crouch. In an instant he scaled the cliff. Bullets hit the rock next to him. Then he felt a searing pain in his shoulder. Almost losing his grip on the rocks, he dug in his heels, pushing with all his might. Reaching the top, he saw Galen with the horses. Leaping up into the saddle, he jerked on the reins, pointed the horse south, booted its side. Both horses flew across the open land, following their basic instinct to home.

Reaching the farm, the two riders guided the animals into the barn. Other men waited, taking the horses from them. Galen picked up a door set into the floor, scooted down with Dray right behind. The heavy wooden door crashed down behind them. Dray could hear the sound of hay being brushed across the opening.

The pain in his back came on stronger, crippling his shoulder. Breathing heavily, Dray followed Galen through the tunnel to an opening, then a passageway. At the first room, they passed, Dray stopped in the doorway. The room was full of children. All different ages, sizes, boys and girls. Several adults sat with them, holding the little ones. None of them cried, but they looked at him with big, wide eyes.

Galen pulled him away, guided him into another room. It held a bed, a man and a woman stood waiting for him. Weakness snuck up on him. He remembered being led to the bed, then darkness.

Rayn

My parents

Everything got mixed up in his head. He felt a mask go over his mouth. Then nothing.

***

Rayn heard the horses gallop across the yard. As they passed the windows, she noticed Dray bent over, a large red stain on the back of his shirt. Luna and Archer came up behind her.

Luna laid her hand on Rayn's shoulder. "Mom, he's hurt."

Rayn nodded, the cutting feeling in her stomach dug deep. Then she heard the dreaded hum of the motorcycles.

They are hot on Galen and Dray's trail.

Archer took hold of Rayn's arm, steering her toward the command room. "Get out of here. We'll handle this."

In a fog of confusion, Rayn obeyed her son-in-law. Running to the command room, Seth pulled her in, shut the wall that hid them.

Inside were Angie and Edward. Rayn glared at Edward. Even though she knew he was caught between a rock and a hard place, his disloyalty still angered her. Folding her arms across her chest, she began to pace. Seth had the largest screen on the wall displaying the scene as it unfolded outside. Rayn watched as Archer and Luna faced off with the troops. The lead officer was not Bono, but a young man about Dray's age.

Rayn stopped pacing, listening to his words.

"Archer, I know they are here. Dray was just at the compound."

Luna stood with her husband. Archer shook his head. "You must be mistaken. Lieutenant Konnor is not here, nor has he been. Why would he? He's the enemy. He doesn't believe in our cause." Archer narrowed his eyes. "And you would be?"

"Lieutenant Milo. Look..." He leaned closer to the couple. "...Dray is my friend. I just want to help him. And end all of this..." He waved his arm wide. "...help me, please."

Rayn narrowed her eyes, sincerity reflected on the man's face.

Archer remained unemotional, his mouth in a tight grin. "Sorry, Sir. I can't help you. He is not here."

Milo straightened up. His face took on the stern look of the officer he was. "I am pretty sure he is wounded. One of the snipers thinks he hit him." Milo's heavy look bore into Archer's face. "We can comb this place and find him..."

"Sir..." The voice of one of the other soldiers sounded behind Milo. "I have blood on the ground." He stood up. "It leads to the barn."

Milo gave Archer a stern look, quickly turned, walking swiftly to where the soldier was kneeing down. Archer and Luna followed a safe distance behind. Milo looked toward the barn. In true military fashion, he marched to the building.

Rayn took in a breath. She turned to face her computer safety-net. "Seth?"

Seth worked his fingers over the keyboard. "Switching cameras."

Rayn looked back at the screen just as Milo entered the barn. The men stopped working. Rayn could see their hands tighten on the tools they held. Innocent when used for the purpose they were created for, deadly when used as weapons.

Milo, followed by four of his men, Luna and Archer, narrowed his eyes and looked around. In a calculated manner, he walked the length of the passageway. His eyes looked down, then up and settled on the floor. He kicked the hay floor with his shiny black boots.

"Frasier..." One of the young soldier jumped to Milo's side.

"Yes Sir."

"Do you see any more blood spots?"

The young man shook his head. "Not really. They seemed to have stopped at the door."

Just then one of the workers came forward, his hand wrapped in a blood stained, white cloth. "Sir, I am afraid the blood is mine. I cut my hand on..." His words were stopped by Milo's sharp, unbelieving the sharp unbelieving glare.

Milo hesitated. Rayn could tell he didn't believe any of it. But, left with no other options, he summoned his men. "Let's go."

As the soldiers retreated from the barn, Milo followed them. Stopping in front of Archer and Luna, Rayn had to strain to hear his words. "I know he is here. I know he thinks he is fighting for a just cause..." He shrugged. "...maybe he is. But General Bono will move heaven and earth to find him..." His eyes went to Luna. "...and Rayn." He bowed, with a click of his heels, turned and left.

Rayn felt a chill go down her spine, as his words and actions reflected what she already knew. She and Dray were the number one target. Wrapping her arms around herself, she shivered.

Things are getting intense. There will have to be a show down. A bloody, violent showdown.

Seth switched the screen back to the front yard. The soldiers turned their bikes to follow Milo. He rode between them, taking over the lead. Closing ranks, the brigade left the farm.

"Rayn." Seth's voice sounded behind her. "Galen is with Dray in the doctor's room."

She turned quickly, walking briskly to the door. Going to the bookcase, she hit the release, it slid open. Bouncing down the stairs, she hurried to get to Dray.

Passing the children in the hall, she slipped quietly in to room where Dray was. Galen met her at the door. "He's lost a lot of blood, but the doc says he's lucky. The wound is high and clean."

Rayn leaned her head on Galen's chest. The weight of nearly losing Dray crashed down on her. She had already buried one man she loved. This war was threatening to take another.

Lord, protect him.

A voice echoed in her soul. **I am. He is learning the truth. He will rise to the challenge.**

Rayn pulled back. Her eyes searched Galen's face. "Dray learned something at the compound..."

Galen nodded. "I know. It is time he knows the truth."

"And that is...?"

Galen's grip tightened on her arms. "It was his parents that Heath met the night he was killed."

CHAPTER TWELVE

The fog surrounded Dray. Fighting to rise to a clear mind, pain radiated from his left shoulder. The memory of the gunshot, the ride to the farm...then darkness. Slowly, he saw through the fog. Turning his head to the right he saw Rayn standing with her back to him. Just seeing her eased the pain, the tightness in his chest.

Licking his dry lips he tried to speak. "Hey."

She turned around, a weak smile formed around her lips. "Hey, soldier." She came to his side, leaned down whispered on his lips. "Didn't they teach you to duck?"

Her eyes were reassuring. He would live. "I guess I wasn't quick enough."

Rayn grabbed a cup on the table next to him, spooned cooling ice chips in his mouth. He licked his lips, the moisture welcome.

Letting the ice melt in his mouth, he took a deep breath. He had not been shot before.

Damn this hurts!

Adjusting the wounded shoulder, he settled down on the hard surface. "Where did they get this mattress? The rock quarry?"

Rayn's lips brushed his. "I see your need for comfort has returned."

With his good arm, he pulled her to him. "I want to be in your bed."

With a twisted smile, she whispered. "You will soon. But for now you need to stay here. They may come back to raid the farm again."

Dray frowned. "Again?"

Rayn nodded. "Yes, a friend of yours, Lieutenant Milo? He came this time."

Dray understood. He had been replaced. He grimaced. "He's a good man...well he was a friend... He gets the job done." He searched Rayn's face. "I think things are going to get intense."

Rayn nodded. "I know, I feel a disturbance in the air."

A heaviness settled over Dray. He needed to sleep. To recharge his energy. To fight the good fight.

He felt Rayn's lips on his, a soft, sweet kiss from the woman he had vowed to protect. Taking her lips into his, he savored the feel, the promise of life after the fight was done.

I promise I will protect you and all you hold dear.

Then the voice whispered. **That you will. Sleep for now, for tomorrow the battle begins.**

***

Galen ran his hand through his hair. The steady breathing of Dray echoed against the sterile white walls. He had sent Rayn up to the house. He needed to talk to Dray. It was a secret he had carried for years. Even Rayn never knew who Heath met the night he died. But Galen was there. The brutal memory of that fateful night jumped from the hidden spaces in his brain.

***

Heath drove the old, beat-up Jeep over the rough ground. Galen hung on the overhead bar as he bounced up off his seat. Two days ago, they received a message from a reliable source. A couple wanted to join. Not a young couple with children, but an older couple with one son. But the son was in the military. In fact, he was being groomed under the guidance of General Bono.

Reaching the meeting point, the two men waited in the darkness, under the cover of the trees. Neither spoke. There was nothing to discuss. They had done this before, but Galen had an uneasy feeling.

The night seemed too still. The moon hid behind dark clouds. A soft, warm mist started to fall. The minutes ticked away. After about an hour, a low beam, single light appeared through the dense brush.

Heath swung out of the vehicle. "Show time."

Galen jumped out. The plan was to take the couple to the farm, hope the Cartel never found out.

Easy peasy!

The couple emerged into the small clearing. The man walked with the stiffness of a military man, dressed in dark green, he was hard to make out. The older woman walked with the sureness of a fit person, dressed in khaki cargo pants and strong walking boots.

Gathering their breath, the couple met the two men halfway.

"Glad to see you two." The man extended his hand. "Ge...Silas Konner. This is my wife, Helena."

Heath took Silas' outstretched hand. "Heath..." with his free hand he pointed his thumb back. "Galen."

Galen stepped forward to greet them. "We need to get out of here. The sooner you are at the farm, the safer you will be..."

Suddenly the clearing was flooded with lights. A faint form walked toward the group. The four faced it together.

The booming voice of General Bono put a shiver of fear down Galen's spine. "General Konnor...Silas. Thanks for bring the Insurgents to me."

Heath jerked sharply to look at Silas. Silas shook his head, returned his focus to Bono. "How did you find us?"

Bono circled the group. Helena was holding her husband's arm, but Galen could see rage in her face. Her body stiff, ready to take on this man.

"Do you honestly think I don't have my ways?" Bono laughed a sinister smirk. "Silly man. I know everything, especially about my men."

Bono stopped his pacing in front of Helena. "My dear, you have a very fine son."

Galen watched as her back bristled, she stepped away from her husband. "Leave him out of it. He knew nothing of this."

Bono chuckled. "Oh, I know. And he will never know of your betrayal as long as he follows commands and is a good soldier."

Galen saw figures moving in the mist. Many, many men advancing toward them. His spirit told him this was bad.

The sound of cocking rifles sent a chill over him. He started backing up, hoping he could make it to the underbrush to hide. He wanted to grab Heath, but the deal was...if danger came, every man for himself.

Bono's words continued, getting fainter..."Now folks, you need to come with us..."

Galen drove into the darkness. Lying on his stomach, he watched as Heath was gunned down by several shots. Another group grabbed Silas and Helena, beating them with the butts of their guns. The couple fell to their knees, still holding hands. The soldiers pulled them apart and drug them toward the lights.

Bono walked over to the still body of Galen's best friend. Kicking him, he motioned for the men standing by to beat on the already dead body. Galen felt tears swell in his eyes, covering his face. Scooting backwards, he covered himself completely. Holding in the sobs, he laid perfectly still.

Bono stood watching the beating in amusement. Then he looked up and around. Galen was afraid he would see him. "Where is the other guy?"

The men stopped, their arms in mid-air. They looked around confused.

Bono stomped his foot. "There was another man with..." He kicked Heath's body. "...this...this...there is another man."

One of the soldiers shook his head. "He must have run away...like the cowards they are!" The other men laughed.

Bono did not. Galen, even far away, could see the doubt in the general's eyes.

Bono looked around again. Finally he shrugged. "Let's go." He commanded.

"But what about this guy?"

Bono spit on Heath's body. "Let the animals have him. He is no longer a threat."

Watching the scene before him, he felt detached. Heath's body lay lifeless, beaten and bleeding. As soon as the sound of the motorcycles and trucks vanished, Galen buried his head in the soft dirt and cried.

***

The cold numbness Galen accepted that night surrounded him. He buried his friend and his feelings. But to honor Heath, he continued to work for the Cause. He also watched Rayn turned her grief inward and go on with the mission she and Heath started.

He was sure that falling in love with Dray disturbed Rayn's soul. But from the moment Galen heard Dray induce himself as Lieutenant Konnor, he knew there was a reason the young man was here. So he waited, never telling Rayn or anyone the connection between Dray and Heath's death.

Galen heard the sheets rustle behind him. Turning, he saw Dray staring at him.

Galen walked over. "How are you doing?"

Dray's eyes fired a spark of mischief. "I've been better." Then his eyes turned serious. "Galen…" He took a breath, raised the bed to a sitting position. "Tell me what happened to my folks."

Galen nodded, pulled a chair over to the bed. Sitting down, he sighed. "Yes. It's time you know."

Retelling the story brought back all the bad emotions. But it was now time to tell.

***

Dray stared at the blank wall in front of him. Galen finished his story, but for every answer there were two more questions. Dray turned to the man. "I was always told they died in a car crash."

Galen faced Dray, he took the question head on. "They weren't in a car."

Dray shook his head. "But I saw them. They were battered and bleeding..." the truth hit him between the eyes. An intense anger over took him so strongly that he shook from the impact. "...that son of a bitch."

He looked away from Galen.

My parents. Rayn's husband. The connection.

Looking down at the tubes in his arm. "So there is a reason I am here."

Galen's words felt like concrete centering the cord of his existence. "Yes, you were destined to come here. I knew it the first day you showed up at the farm. Your mother wanted you to know your children, her grandchildren."

"You know I have a daughter about to be born?"

Galen nodded. "Yes. How do you feel about that?"

Dray chuckled. "Pretty good." He looked up at Galen. "It was strange. When Tesla told me, I had this overwhelming feeling of joy. Odd, huh?"

Galen put his hands in his pockets, rocked back on his heels. "No, it's how you should feel."

All of this was a lot to absorb.

Dray had never believed, nor even thought about a deeper meaning to life. It was what it was. Now he had feelings and emotions that bombarded him. A mother who gave her life to try and protect him, a father who stood with her, a child-a daughter, a lover who lost her husband trying to right a wrong. And now, a belief that there was a higher purpose.

Dray shook his head to clear it.

Galen placed his hand on Dray's arm. "Don't try to figure it all out at once. It is like a wheel in motion, what goes around comes around."

As stupid as Dray once thought those words were, now they made sense. He nodded, placed his hand over Galen's, looked the man in the eyes. "I am beginning to understand, no..." He shook his head. "...that's not true. I don't understand any of this. But it feels right. Does that make sense?"

Galen chuckled. "Yes, it does."

Dray had a nagging thought tugging at him. "Rayn...Heath...I feel bad she lost her husband...but..." He looked Galen dead in the eyes. "...I love her. Is that all right?"

Galen smiled. "I am pretty sure it is. Otherwise it wouldn't have happened."

The words comforted Dray. He could accept all of this weirdness, but not being able to love Rayn? That he couldn't bear.

**

With the patience of a saint, Dray waited while the nurse took the needles and tubes out of his body. His arm still tingled with pain, but it wasn't anything he couldn't handle.

Doc Brody stood in the doorway. "You're good Dray. Keep it in the sling for another day, then just work it. Easy at first, but you are young. You will heal."

Dray flexed the fingers on his injured arm. "Thanks Doc." Free to move off the bed, he swung his legs over the edge. Now he could get dressed and get back to the task at hand. Since speaking with Galen, he knew now what his focus should be. And General Bono was going down. One way or another.

Standing alone in the room, he awkwardly buttoned his shirt with one hand. He heard the door push open. His face lit up.

Rayn

He smiled at her. "Will you help here?"

Rayn walked over, began buttoning his shirt. He took in her scent of clean linen. Since he had time to clear his mind, he accepted the way things were. And enjoyed the things that made him feel alive, like loving Rayn did.

She patted his chest. "There you go soldier." She reached up and kissed him. "How are you feeling?"

Dray shrugged. "Pretty good for being shot." With his good arm he pulled her into him. Kissing her, he lingered, allowing the sweet feeling of loving her wash over him. Accepting that this was all a plan, he felt the freedom to love her.

Wrapping her arms around his neck, she formed into his body. "I've missed you."

"Never again will we separated."

"Promise?"

"Yes, I promise." He released her, took her hand. "Now, let's get to Seth and find out how he is doing."

Rayn nodded. "I do know that getting the code helped."

Walking down the underground hallway, they surfaced in the dining room. Going straight to the command room, they found Seth and Edward working away at their computers. At the sound of the sliding doors, both turned toward the couple.

Seth greeted them. "Hey, Lie...Dray. How are you doing?"

Dray slapped Seth on the back. "Good." He turned his attention to Edward. "How's it going?"

Edward sighed. "It's good for us, I am just worried about my mom and sister. If the Cartel finds out about them..."

Dray nodded. "I know, hopefully we can get them out before it becomes apparent that you are on our side?" Dray left it at a question, waiting for Edward's answer.

Edward met Dray's stare dead on. "Yes, I am on your side. I just want my family here so we can work together, for you."

Dray studied Edward. Satisfied that the man was being up front, he looked back at Seth's screen. "So, what's happening?"

Seth smiled. "When we have the code activated, we can track them. We sent them west, but some held back. I think General Bono is still at the compound. It seems Lieutenant Milo has taken your place." Seth looked up at Dray, waiting for his reaction.

Dray nodded. Seth went on. "So... the good lieutenant is on his way back. I expect Bono or Milo here soon. A couple of days at most."

Rayn stepped around back of Dray. He looked to his side, watching her. She studied the two screens. Dray compared them. While on different sites, they didn't seem to bring anything that would alarm him.

Rayn shifted her weight from one leg to both. "Edward..." the young man's hand froze. "Do you know where your people are?"

Edward spoke quietly. "Yes ma'am. My mom is working in the kitchen. Nora, my sister, is in the computer room."

Rayn folded her arms across her chest. "She a computer geek like you?"

"Yes, ma'am."

"Can you find her computer?"

Edward blushed. "I'm trying. I know she is scared to respond, but I am hoping she can send me some kind of signal."

Rayn nodded. "Keep trying." She turned to Dray. "I need to check on some things. Catch you later."

Dray watched her leave.

What was that all about?

He turned back to find Seth and Edward staring at him. He shrugged. "I don't know. But do as she says. I am sure she has a reason."

***

Something triggered a spark of a memory for Rayn. She needed to get back outside, to feel the openness, to explore her thoughts.

The tattoo on her arm flamed, sending sparks. Luckily she wore a sleeveless top or it would have ignited. The flaming didn't frighten her as far as being burned. It was an alarm to warn her of coming events.

The wind rustled the leaves of the oak tree she stood under. Rayn raised her arms, the sparks hitting her cheek, but it didn't burn. Instead, it was like a powdery mist. The strong smell of Frankincense overcame her. Calming her, helping her reach a meditative state, it reminded her of the inside of a church

129

The familiar voice spoke low. **It is coming into being.**

What is it? Her words were spoken in her mind not out loud.

The unrest in the souls of the righteous.

Is that what I feel?

Yes, you need to brace yourself. It will get worse before it gets better.

Worse than it is now? Rayn sighed.

Yes, but know this. You will rise victorious.

And everything has a price. What is mine?

Your heart. You will lose your heart.

Rayn stood silent. Could she suffer the loss of another loved one? Is that what it was asking of her?

No, that is not what I am asking.

Rayn frowned. *What are you asking?*

Trust in the love I have sent you. He is groomed to be a warrior. His heart is pure, his soul secured, his spirit guided by love from his parentage.

Rayn had a stray thought, but heard the grass crunching down behind her. She turned to see Dray walking toward her. The sunbeams outlined his body. An invisible pat on her shoulder told her all she needed to know.

"Hey, Lady. Are you okay?" Dray closed the distance between them.

Rayn nodded her head. "I am now. I just needed some air to clear my head." She ran her hand up his arm, feeling the heat from his tattoo. While not as hot as hers, she knew it was giving him the power to stand strong.

He took hold of her arms. "What sent you away so quickly?"

Rayn's mind was blank, then the thought jumped into her head. "Edward."

"What about him?"

"He's still scared of the Cartel. He trusts us, but his heart is breaking for fear he will do something that will cause them to hurt his family." Rayn felt her spirit jump. "We need to help him."

Dray pulled back to look at her. "Where is this coming from?"

Rayn knew the answers. "In my heart. He is a good soul, he thinks of his family first." Burying her face in his body, she soaked up the smell of him, of passion and depth. It gave her strength.

Looking around, Dray frowned. "Is the Rock here?" He turned his look back to her. "Isn't that where the epiphanies are?"

Rayn chuckled. "They can come wherever."

"So tell me your Divine revelation?"

Rayn scrunched up her mouth. "Edward needs to know we can keep his mother and sister safe."

"Can we?"

"Yes, we can."

"And he doesn't know this?"

"Not in his heart of hearts."

"So we do what...?"

Rayn paused for a second, then stepped back. "Let's go talk to Edward." Taking his hand, she moved toward the house. Leading him up the stairs, they reentered the computer room. Releasing his hand, she walked to Edward. Placing her hands on his shoulders, she felt his muscles tighten. He looked up at her, suspicion creased his eyes.

Rayn spoke with a low, but powerful authority. "Edward. Your family is safe. We will get them out of there. But they need your help now, we need you to help us break through the code. That is the way we help them."

She turned his chair toward her, knelt down so they were eye level. "Talk to me."

Edwards's words came out muted, choppy. "I...am one..." He looked up at Dray and Seth. "...step away from entering their site." Edward's frown showed doubt.

Rayn went on. "Find them. I have people inside to keep them safe."

Edward nodded, his eyes filling with water. Rayn stood up, placed her hands on his shoulders as he faced the computer. Tapping the keys, when he hit 'ENTER' the screen became flooded with letters, numbers and characters. The large screens on the walls copied the jumble of mixed fonts.

Seth shouted as the room turned into a maze of digits flowing over the walls. "We're in!"

Rayn patted Edward's shoulders as the images bounced from wall to wall, ceiling to floor. "Good job. Find your family."

CHAPTER THIRTEEN

In a clockwise motion, Rayn wiped the fog from the mirror. Just finishing her shower, she shook her hair, watching her reflection in the clear round space. So much had happened in the last few days. So many memories had come to the surface. But she carried an unrest in her spirit. Dray was a welcome addition to the Cause, but he also presented a bigger danger. Bono was dead set on finding him to make him pay for deserting.

Wrapping a towel around her still moist body, she walked into the bedroom. Dray was working on some papers at the desk. He was wearing a pair of sweat bottoms, Rayn leaned against the door watching him work. The sight of him sent a shiver down her body. She never expected to love again after Heath died. The path had been clear in her mind–follow the mission, protect the children, defeat the Cartel.

The first time Dray rode up on his bike, she felt a physical attraction. His manner and style drew her in. But she swiped the thoughts from her mind. She had a job to do. But somehow they seemed to connect on the same level, even though they were coming from different places. She fought the feelings, until he helped her escape. Coming to know his true spirit, the attraction became real. There was something missing, a bit of information, something.

Dray looked up. "Hey." His eyes slide down her body. "You look refreshed."

She narrowed her eyes. Stayed at the doorway.

Dray picked up on her vibes. "I need to tell you something."

A feeling of dread rose up from her gut. She nodded.

Dray stood, walked around the desk, but kept his distance. "I just found out that it was my parents that your husband met the night they were..." His hesitation changed his tone. "...killed."

Shockwaves crashed over her. The words from today echoed in her mind.

His heart is pure, his soul secured, his spirit guided by love from his parentage.

"How do you know? Did you just find out? At the compound?"

Dray half sat, half leaned on the desk's edge. "Yes. I confronted General Bono. He told me..." His eyes searched hers for understanding. "...Galen confirmed it."

Rayn pushed off from the door jamb. Confusion clouded her reasoning. "So your folks wanted to join the residence?"

Dray shrugged. "I guess so...I never knew anything about it." He rose away from the desk. Standing in the middle of the room, his body wanted to step toward her. But she watched as his mind struggled against it.

This was a mindblower, but it also made sense.

He was brought here for a reason. Not just for the animal lust, but for the accountability to his parents.

Shutting the door behind her, she walked over to him. Holding her towel with one hand, she stroked his cheek with the other. "Now I understand why you are here. It was put out to the universe by your folks to be on our side."

He kissed the palm of her hand. "It kind of blew me away, but then again it brings everything I am feeling into place."

Rayn leaned her head close to his. "So, you are finishing what they started?"

Dray nodded. "For some unknown reason, when Galen told me, it gave me peace." He pulled her into him. "I can see clearly now what I need to do."

"And that is?"

"Fight the Cartel and..." He bit his lower lip, pulled back to look at her. "...and protect my daughter, the granddaughter of Silas and Helene."

The words set Rayn free as she knew they did Dray. Letting go of her towel, she melted into him.

He growled, lifted her up, carried her to the bed. Laying her gently down, he came to her with a new abandonment. She accepted him. Now she felt their souls were seared together.

Her body ached for him. Coming together as comrades and fellow believers these last few days, made this night special. Also, letting go of her guilt for loving someone after Heath finally made sense to her. Life went on, the living needed to extend out to others. Reaching out to Dray made perfect logic now.

Touching the cool blue tattoo as she ran her hands up his arms, she felt sexual desire spark inside of her. An easy, but passionate trigger. As their skin touched, her defenses released, opening up her body and her heart. Allowing the ecstasy of loving this man engulfed her. His lips moved over her, sending a frenzy of dizzying pleasure to her core.

A warm summer breeze blew through the open window. The night sounds welcomed the lovers. She knew she was in one with the Earth and Dray.

A gripping orgasm exploded her peaceful thoughts. Sending a riveting spasm up, she muffled her screams as this was the most powerful one yet. He entered her slowly, then his hardness grew, creating a friction sending her over again. Feeling his shutter, she grasped ahold of him, holding the lingering contentment. Their sweaty bodies smelted together. Ryan closed her eyes to keep the moment as long as she could.

The wind cooled their overly aroused bodies. Feeling him move on her, she opened her eyes.

Dray looked down at her. "It was different this time?"

She nodded. "Yes."

"Why?" He wiped the moisture from her forehead.

"Because we are now connected by a past and a future."

Dray rolled away from her. She moved backwards into the curve of his body. His words tickled her neck. "And that makes a difference?"

Rayn wiggled into him. "It does. It is all clear now."

He wrapped his arms over her bare breasts. "Tell me how."

"We were destined to meet, to work together, to be victorious over the evil."

His voice was low, filled with a recognition she never heard from him before. "I can accept that now."

She snuggled closer. "Do you have a choice?"

Sighing, he tightened his hold. "I am thinking not."

***

Dray finished his coffee in one gulp. He need to do some kind of physical work today. Even his injured shoulder ached to move, he needed to move it. He was wound tighter that a clock spring. Finding out the truth about his parents, knowing the connection between them and Rayn's husband, he had a new respect for the work going on here. This was a well-orchestrated plan that was guided by divine powers.

Divine powers!! Who would have thought I would be guided by divine powers.

Brushing pass the other people, he had spent enough time with computers, hackers and black screens filled with white lettering.

No, he needed to fill the sun on his back. Sweat, from something other than love-making, on his face. There was always something to do outside. Skipping over the rough ground, his feet hit gravel, then the wooden floor of the barn. Dander from the hay assaulted his nose. He sneezed twice. Casper walked up to him, handed him a white handkerchief.

Dray nodded. "Thanks."

The man cocked his head to the side. "What are you doing out here?"

Dray stuffed the cloth in his pocket. "Looking for something to do."

"Really?" Dray saw the skeptical look in the man's eyes.

Sticking out his hand, Dray smiled a weak smile. "Really..."

Casper ignored the out-stretched hand.

Dray wiped his palm on his jeans. "Is that a problem?"

Casper narrowed his eyes, studying Dray for a minute. Dray waited, not knowing what he would do if his offer was refused.

Go quietly back to the house with his tail between his legs?

Casper nodded. "No problem. What can you do?"

Dray's heart jumped. "Whatever you need."

"We need wood for the winter. Can you chop wood?"

Dray shrugged. He had chopped wood at the cabin.

This I can do.

"Sure."

Casper frowned. "What about your shoulder?"

Dray moved it up and down, camouflaging the pain with a smile.

Casper pointed towards the back door. "Out back. Everything you need is there."

Dray shook with the excitement of being accepted. Whistling he passed rows and rows of animals. Horses, cows, pigs. All were in their own stalls.

Swinging by the last stall, he turned back to see Casper watching him. "How come all the animals are inside?" He waved his hand toward the open doors.

"Storm's coming." Casper switched his weight to the other leg.

Dray stepped out into the sunlight. "Really? How do you kn..." He stopped mid-sentence. "Never mind."

Going to the unchopped pile of tree branches and stumps, he removed his shirt, put on the leather gloves. Yanking the ax out of the chopping block.

This would do the trick.

Placing the first log upright, he swung the ax. It hit the wood and spilt the log.

Nice.

***

Tesla walked over the uneven ground, heading for the barn. The weight of her pregnancy rode on her lower back. Locking her fingers under her stomach relieved some of the pressure.

"Little one, you need to make your appearance soon." Tesla spoke low, addressing her belly. "You're killing me here." The warm summer morning smiled on the mother and child. Walking into the barn she ran into Casper.

He steadied her with his hands. "Where you off to in such a hurry, child?"

She smiled. "I think I will take Battle Scar out for a ride." Battle scar was her favorite horse. Wounded as a colt by the Cartel, he wore his name proudly.

Casper glanced down at her belly. "Are you sure this is a good idea?"

Tesla frowned. "Yeah, why not?"

"There's a storm rolling in."

"I know I feel it, but it's a ways out." She smiled at him. "Help me, will ya'?"

Casper took her hand, led her to one of the stalls. The jet black horse raised its head, snorted at the visitors.

Casper went to the gate, as Tesla patted the nose of the welcoming animal. While he saddled Battle Scar, Tesla talked softly to mighty animal. "Hey, boy. We need to get out and about for a while. And if you could convince the baby girl to come out." She relished the smells of leather, hay and horse hair.

Tesla stepped back as Casper put the halter over the horse's ears. As he led the horse out of the stall, Tesla stood back, turning as the animal cleared the gate.

Reaching for the horn of the saddle, she struggled to pull her heavy weight up. Suddenly, she felt a hand on her butt, pushing. Giving her the needed boost, she swung up and mounted.

Sitting tall in the saddle, she took up the reins. "Thanks Casper. Hopefully, soon I won't need help getting on a horse.

Laying the leather against the horse's neck, she allowed him to trot out the back of the barn.

Hearing the crack of wood startled Battle Scars. The stallion snorted, then side-stepped. Tesla looked over toward the sound, surprised to see Dray, his shirt off, the sweat glistening off his muscular chest. She took in a breath. His physique still made her mouth water. She always enjoyed seeing Dray. He was one hunk of a man.

Dray stopped long enough to recognize the rider. "Tesla." He frowned. "Are you supposed to be riding?"

She smiled at his concern. "It's all right if I take it easy, I have ridden all my life."

Dray walked over to her. "Really? I didn't know that."

Tesla grimaced. "We don't know much about each other, do we?"

Dray rested his hand on the horse's neck. "No, we don't." He looked at her bulging belly. "How is she doing?"

Tesla rubbed her free hand over her stomach. "She is good. Just taking her sweet time to make her appearance."

She could see her words affected him. She reached down took his hand, placed it on her lower belly. "Can you feel her?"

At that moment the baby kicked, Tesla saw Dray's hand move, the look of astonishment on his face.

Dray spoke to the lump moving under his hand. "Ready to meet you baby girl." He looked up at Tesla. "Have a good ride." His glaze softened with concern. "Be careful. A storm is coming."

Tesla picked up the reins as Dray moved back. "So I've been told." Steering the stallion toward the open field, she tossed over her shoulder. "See you later."

Giving the horse full rein, she rode with the ease of an experienced rider. Sitting tight in the saddle, she relished the wind that hit her face.

While things were not as she wished, that Dray would come, scoop her up, make them a family, things were all right. Her daughter would be born with her father the first person she saw. Tesla couldn't imagine anything better. At least Dray would be part of her life.

A cold chill crossed Tesla's back. Pulling up Battle Scar, she found the sky full of dark, opaque clouds. The horse let out a harsh, piercing whinny, raising his head towards the east. Without Tesla's guidance, he bolted toward the rough terrain.

"Whoa, Battle Scar!" Tesla screamed into the wind.

The animal paid no attention. At a dead run, he toppled over the uneven rocks and bumps. Tesla dropped the reins, gripped the saddle horn as a stabbing pain rocked her body.

"Not now baby!!" Fear gripped her chest.

A bolt of lightning hit the ground next to them. Battle Scar stumbled, throwing Tesla from the saddle. She had tried to hold on, but her hands slipped from the wet leather. Hitting the ground with a thump, her head snapped against a rock.

About to lose consciousness, she felt a knife-like pain cut through her belly. Screaming to the sky. "Help me, please." She felt a darkness at the edge of her awareness, she needed to do something.

Battle Scar nudged her with his nose. The wetness brought her mind back into present. "Go...get...Dray." Tesla managed to say before the darkness took over completely. She barely heard the hoof beats faintly fade.

***

Dray watched as Tesla rode away. He cared for her.
She is the mother of my child.
But he felt a great regret that he did not love her.
Can't change that.
He swung the ax, resumed splitting the wood. Throwing two logs on the growing pile, he wiped his brow with the back of his glove.
This was a good idea.

His mind cleared, his purpose becoming clearer. And seeing Tesla only confirmed his convictions. He was led here for a reason. And the reason was nobler than anything he had done in his life.

Returning to his chore, he lost track of the time. Suddenly, he heard a crack of thunder. Stopping, he looked up at the sky. Dark, ominous clouds lumped together. A heavy wind blew through the trees. In the distance, he saw a form coming toward him. Laying down the ax, he removed his gloves. Grabbing his shirt he slipped it on. Figuring it was Tesla, he was glad she was coming back.

Before he could button his shirt, Battle Scar galloped up to him. Dray grabbed hold of the flying reins. "Whoa, boy." He pulled the horse to a stop.

Dray heard Casper's voice behind him. "Tesla. Where is she?"

Dray looked at the riderless horse. "Something must have happened." He swung up into the saddle. "Go, boy take me to Tesla."

The horse rose on its back legs, took off toward the distance. Dray bent down, riding close to the horse's neck. Allowing the animal to follow his instincts, Dray became aware of a heavy rain falling over them. The rolling clouds thundered, raised high, hanging low. A flash of light hit the ground on the horizon.

Suddenly, the horse turned east. Riding across the rain, Dray shook the cooling water from his hair.

Up a small bluff, Battle Scar slipped on the ground that had now turned to mud. Dray held on to the saddle horn, as his body slipped from side to side.

Abruptly, the stallion stopped. Dray almost flew over the top of the horse's head. Looking around he saw Tesla's body lying a few feet down an embankment. Jumping from the horse, Dray slipped down to her.

Her face was gray, he swollen body drenched. Reaching her, he took hold of her hand, shouting her name over the noise of the storm.

"Tesla!"

Oh, God, let her be alive.

At that moment, her eyes flew open, she screamed. Her grip on his hand intensified. "Dray. I am in labor."

"Oh shit." The panic rose in his throat. "No! You can't be!"

"Not up for discussion." She spoke through clenched teeth.

Without thinking, he lifted her up, carried her to the waiting horse. Half throwing her up on the back of the horse, he mounted. "Grab hold of me."

He felt her arms go around him. He kicked the side of the horse, turning him toward the farm. "Go home, boy. Quickly." It was as if the horse understood. Breaking into a smooth run, the horse carried the couple swiftly toward the farm.

Dray felt Tesla's arms tighten around him, heard her moan, he figured it was a contraction. That was the most he knew of labor. With a relieved sigh, he saw the barn rise from the skyline. Battle Scar carried the two of them into the shelter of the building.

Casper greeted them. "What happened?" He grabbed hold of the halter, stopped the moving animal.

Two other men appeared, took Tesla from the saddle. Carrying her, another man opened the trap door that Dray had gone down when he was shot.

He followed them through the hallway, to the sterile white room. Doc Brody motioned toward the empty bed. "What happened?"

Dray was trying to catch his breath. "I think she fell off the horse. She's in labor."

The Doc bend over her. "Tesla, talk to me."

The young girl lay quietly. As if instructed, the nurse placed a mask over her nose, the doctor placed her legs in the metal stirrups.

Dray walked to Tesla's side. "Tesla, she's coming."

Nothing.

The lights flickered, went coal black. Dray felt panic rise in his chest. Then a dim set of lights started to glow, brighter still until he could see

Tesla was still, her hands limp at her side.

Dray shouted at the doctor. "What's wrong?"

Doc Brody didn't answer. He barked directions at the nurse. "She's coming."

All Dray could see was blood. He took hold of Tesla cold hand. The feeling alarmed him. But his attention went back to the bloody blob the doctor pulled from Tesla's body. It screamed and for some reason it was the best sound Dray had ever heard.

He shook Tesla hand. "She's here. She's beautiful. Look..." as he turned away from the sight of his daughter, he knew he was speaking to a dead person. Caressing her face, he whispered. "Oh, Tesla. I am so sorry." He looked back at the blanketed bundle in the nurse's arms. "I will take care of her, I promise."

The nurse held the baby out to him. Releasing Tesla's lifeless hand, he gathered his daughter to his chest. Holding the warm bundle, he couldn't help but smile.

The nurse spoke at his elbow. "Do you have a name?"

A glow of light circled the small child's head. "Halo. Her name is Halo." He turned to look back at her mother and saw the doctor pull a sheet over her face.

He felt helpless, alone and sad. So very sad. The baby in his arms moved. He looked down at his daughter.

So I am on my own.

"You are not alone." The nurse laid her hand on his arm. "We have lots of people to help you."

***

The storm raged up top. The winds whipped the trees, breaking branches, uprooting others. Rayn stood at the opening to the underground, helping as the adults ushered the children down to safety.

Once the bookcase closed, she ran to the computer room. The screens on the wall flashed, went black, then flashed again.

Seth, Edward and Angie were at their stations, trying to keep the data stable. Suddenly, the room went pitch black. Rayn stood still. No one spoke. Then the lights came on.

Seth shook his head, speaking to Rayn over his shoulder. "We need to shut down or we will lose everything."

Rayn walked up behind him. "How bad is it?"

"Bad." His words spoken with a quiet resolve. "It's reads like a tornado. The backup generator has kicked on, but..."

"Shut 'em down." Rayn turned at the sound of the doors sliding open.

Galen entered, along with Archer and Luna.

Seth concurred. "Good idea." At his words, the screens started going black one by one.

Archer looked over Seth's shoulder. "How big is the system?"

"Three or four hours. It is just getting started." Seth kept his computer on.

Rayn turned to Galen. "Where's Dray?"

"He's down below."

Rayn frowned. "What's wrong?"

Galen tightened his lips. "Tesla went into labor."

"That should be a good thing?"

"It should, but I don't think things is going good."

Rayn was torn. She wanted to go comfort Dray, but she needed to be up top monitoring the weather. Stepping into her logic, she deduced. Dray was safe below. Whatever happened, there would be plenty of time to deal with it.

She nodded to Galen. "So, what is the damage so far?"

"A tree hit the south side of the barn. The animals are safe. Casper got them all secure."

Archer spoke up. "The wind ripped off part of the roof over the kitchen. Piper is dealing with the water coming in. Nothing we can do until it passes."

Luna walked over to her mom. "The children are safe below..."

A loud crack made all of them jerk around. Seth shut off his computer, threw his hands up. "Done. Shutting down." His screen went black. The steady hum of all the machines was silenced.

Galen looked toward the closed door. "That sounded like the glass in front."

Rayn bolted out of the room, the others followed. In the front area a huge tree had broken the large glass window. Rain and wind whipped around the now exposed room. Galen and Archer fought the powerful fury of leaves and driving water to get to the fallen branch. Together, they pushed it back out the window. Shattered glass and debris littered the room. Open to the elements, the room looked like a war zone.

With the storm still gathering power, there was nothing they could do for now. The four stood back against the wall, blocking as much of the pelting rain they could. Stepping back into a small foyer, they each took up spot on the floor. Seth, Edward and Angie remained in the computer room. In true geek form, they would protect the machines.

Rayn leaned back against the wall, drawing her knees to her chest. The pounding of the storm seemed to grow. It could destroy so much. She sighed. They had secured as much as they could. It was a waiting game.

***

The sirens in the Fort alerted the people to seek shelter in the underground rooms. General Bono stomped down the hall, shouting commands. Lieutenant Milo directed the people in the offices to the safe havens, downstairs. He knew the general would be of little help.

"I'm going down." Bono flashed by Milo.

Milo smiled.

First one down.

Milo walked the now empty halls. The walls quaked with the impact of the storm. Checking rooms to make sure they were empty, he left the building. Fighting a driving rain, he went to the first building on the left. This was where they kept the children.

He was greeted by the director. "Lieutenant Milo?"

Milo looked around. "Elliot. Are the children safe?"

Elliot nodded. "Yes, we have them in the shelter." His eyes betrayed his mistrust. "Is there a problem?"

Milo narrowed his eyes. "No problem, if you have done as you have been directed. You have, I assume."

Elliot puffed up. "But of course, Sir."

"Good, take me below."

"But Sir..." a large clap of thunder jolted the doors.

Milo raised one eyebrow.

Elliot bowed. "Of course, Sir." He waved his arm toward a metal door. "This way."

Milo lead the way. Going down the steps, the steel heels on his boots hit the metallic stairs with a clicking sound. He could heard the softer footsteps of the director.

Milo had never been fond of Elliot. The stern little man seemed to take pleasure in riding roughshod over small children and the lowly helpers. He just wanted to make sure they were all safe.

The electric lights flickered, went dark, then came on. Subtle at first then gathering brightness. Milo heard Elliot gasp as he bumped into a wall. He shook his head.

Idiot!

Reaching the only door at the end of the walkway, Milo turned the lever. Opening to dimness, his eyes adjusted. Then he saw them. Children of all ages, dressed in the standard gray uniforms. Each sitting on the floor, cross-legged, faces blank. No fear, but no solace either. Milo wonder what they felt.

Elliot cleared his throat behind him. Milo nodded. "Looks good, Elliot..." He turned and patted the man's shoulder as he passed. "Keep them safe."

Elliot's "Yes, sir." faded as Milo left the room. Walking back down the hallway to the stairs, the only sound he heard was his own footsteps. Opening the last solid door, he was assaulted by a strong gust, flying glass. He covered his face with his arm. Pushing against the mighty current of air, he finally reached the door leading outside. But there was no door. Just a metal frame with shards of glass remaining.

Knocking down the remaining glass with his elbow, he stepped carefully through the frame. Being half carried by the wind, he half ran to the building that housed the computers. Using all his strength, he pulled the solid steel door open. Jumping inside, he allowed the door to slam shut behind him. An eerie feeling flooded over him. Memories of the unexplained storm in the plains seemed to connect with the storm outside.

The quiet of the building was welcome. All looked well.

CHAPTER FOURTEEN

When a storm releases all its energy, the world draws inside to protect itself. The farm and the compound tried its best to stand against Nature's assault. It succeed to a certain point. While the structures received damage, the people were safe.

Some event had set a powerful wave across the land. Trees, forced to bow in reverence, the wind sings a song of prevailing potential power as the earth welcomed the strength of the lightning storm.

For hours, they waited until the storm was spent, settling down to a gentle rain and peaceful sky.

One by one, the people of the compound and the farm dared to step out of their harbors. Checking for damage, they were all relieved that the storm had passed. Why nature decided to rage, was a mystery. But they accepted it was over for now.

But in reality it was just the beginning.

***

Rayn sat, knees pulled up to her chest, her head buried in her arms. The other people with her stirred. She raised her head, looked over at Galen.

His eyes met hers. "Where is Dray?"

Galen narrowed his eyes. "In the medic room."

Rayn untangled her body. Stretching, she came to her feet. As the rest of the group stood, she walked to the front area. While the room looked destroyed, she could tell it was significant damage.

Walking over to the bookcase, she hit the latch. As it slid back, she addressed Galen. "I need to see Dray."

He nodded to her.

Down the steps to the long hallway, she passed the children and caretakers as they surfaced. Hugging the wall, she made her way to the med room. Entering, she paused at the doorway, looked around. The room seemed empty. Everything in its proper place. Hearing a creak, she looked to her left, saw Dray rocking in a chair, holding a small blanketed bundle.

He looked up at her, a small smile creased his lips. "Hey."

Rayn went over to him, squatted down. Touching the blanket, she felt movement. "Hey."

Dray opened the wrap, raising the baby so Rayn could see her. "This is my daughter, Halo."

Rayn knew immediately why the storm and its meaning. She moved the blanket away from the baby's right arm. The small tattoo of the power glowed.

Dray stared at the sight. "I didn't see that." He looked to Rayn. "What does it mean?"

Rayn stroked the tiny arm. "It means she was chosen." She looked up at Dray. "What happened here?"

"Well, Tesla went for a ride on Battle Scar, then the storm. The horse came back without her...I found her on the ground, unconscious." He frowned. "I brought her back, but..." He took a deep breath. "She died."

Rayn rested her hand on his arm. "I'm sorry. But Halo looks good."

Dray looked down at his daughter. "She is, isn't she?" He leaned down, kissed the small head.

Rayn watched the two.

Would he understand that this was a special child?
The voice answered her.

He will. It just isn't forthcoming to him yet.

Rayn looked up to see the nurse enter. She went to Dray. "I need to feed her. And..." She frowned at him. "...You need to take a shower and get some rest."

Dray chuckled as he handed the baby up to the nurse's waiting arms. "I suppose. When can I see her again?"

The nurse cuddled the baby. "Anytime you want."

Dray stood, staring at the empty space the nurse left. He stretched his hand out to Rayn, pulling her up to him.

They left the room, walked down the hall to the stairs. Stepping back to allow her go ahead of him, he asked the burning question. "What happened up there?"

Rayn kept climbing. "I'll tell you all about it."

***

Lieutenant Milo had ridden out the storm in the computer room. The echo on the radar reflected the intensity of the energy descending over the Fort. Never had he seen such a display of swirling colors to track the weather. Then they disappeared. The screen turned clear.

The quiet bothered him more than the noise of the storm. He could feel it in the room filled with computers, turned off and silent. But more than that, he could feel it in his body. Leaving the room quickly, he took the stairs two at a time, shoving against the metal door. The sunlight hit his eyes in a burst. While there was glass and debris shattered over the building, it still stood.

Carefully avoiding the broken pieces of debris, he stepped outside. Looking up, the sky was a clear blue. He went directly to the office building. Opening the door to the underground, he yelled. "All clear."

He stood at the side as one by one the people emerged, hesitate at first. Even the hardened soldiers were weary of the storm. General Bono emerged mid-stream. Shaking off his cowardice, he huffed off to his office. Milo stayed to make sure everyone was okay. As the crowd moved through the halls, he heard gasps as the damage was surveyed.

Milo sighed, walked to the general's office. Entering, he saw Bono at his computers, punching the keys, a grave frown on his face.

Finally, he released a deep breath, leaned back in the chair. "I see the system survived."

Milo stood at attention. "Yes Sir. The tech crew did a good job of protecting the network."

Bono looked up from his screen. "So what was that? A tornado? Cyclone? And act of God?"

It took everything Milo had to not react to the last assumption. "Probably all three. I have never seen anything like it."

Bono narrowed his eyes. "You have a thought?"

Milo shook his head. "No Sir." Which was a lie. Milo had many thoughts. Mainly that something distinctive happened in the Universe, bringing the Earth to its feet, so to speak.

"Go check on everything." Bono's abrupt dismissal meant he didn't want to know.

Milo bowed. "On it Sir." Snapping around, he ground his teeth. Marching out the building, he saw the workers removing the broken and bent pieces of many structures. Stopping for a moment, he allowed the quiet to infiltrate his soul. It spoke of a phenomenon that had occurred in the last few hours.

A child. It whispered.

Milo frowned. First, at the inter voice. Second, the message.

A child. What does that mean?

***

Dray found sleep a welcome relief. His mind and body were exhausted from the events of the last few hours. He was a father. And some kind of storm had racked over the land. Somehow, he felt there was a connection, but his mind was too mushy to understand. He allowed his whole being to escape into the slumber of the weary.

Awaking from his dreamless siesta, he lay there for a minute letting his mind focus on the preceding occurrences. His daughter had come into the world in the midst of a mighty storm. As he had held her, he could feel the turbulence from above ground in his spirit.

And the tattoo? He had to earn his. Why was Halo born with one?

The small being was too fragile to battle. She would become strong. He could do that for her. But now?

152

She is stronger in her spirit than you can even imagine.
Dray sat up, giving himself a head rush.
Are you fucking kidding me?
You should have learnt by now, I don't kid.
But she is just a baby.
Then care for her, make her a strong warrior.
A warrior?

Dray jumped out of bed, went to the window. The yard was full of people clearing away fragments of the storm, repairing broken structures. But his eyes went to the rich blue heavens. On the horizon, he saw a double rainbow. Not natural for a sunny sky. However, he understood it was not his to know, or reason. It was for his daughter.

Standing for a moment with what little reasonable thoughts he possessed, he bowed his head in reverence to a Power greater than anything he had ever known.

He had a sudden urge to see Halo. Pulling on clean jeans and a shirt from the closet, he dashed downstairs. Stopping long enough in the kitchen to grab a cup of coffee from Piper, he ran down the hideaway stairs. He stopped suddenly at the bottom.

Where was she?

Passing several rooms, he glanced in. Finally he found a room that housed small cribs. Walking in, he immediately saw her. Going to the single bassinet, he stood over her gazing down. In his mind he saw visions of his mother and Tesla. A sadness came over him. These strong women would never see this child.

Don't count on it.

Dray smiled as he touched his daughter's soft cheek. He was getting used to the voice in his head. Actually found comfort in it.

Reaching down, he scooped up Halo. Her eyes opened, he could swear she smiled. Looking around he found a rocking chair in the corner. Sitting down, he hummed a familiar tune. He didn't know where it came from, but he was quietly reaching the point where things just happened.

153

Rayn pulled the damaged board from the window. She had seen Dray fly by, into the kitchen, then down the steps. She knew better than to stop him. He had a place he needed to be, she had work to do.

The arrival of Halo had set the heavens and Earth into a massive tailspin. Now she knew how things were connected, why they came into being.

"Rayn?" Galen's voice cut though her thoughts.

Regaining her senses, she shook her head. "Yes?"

"I was asking, what do you think happened here? I mean the storm and everything?"

Rayn looked at her dear friend. "I don't know, but I feel...it's a message."

Luna and Archer came up behind Galen.

"What's the message?" Luna frowned at her mother's words.

Rayn shook her head, then lifted her chin. "It is coming around. We need to prepare for a battle...and..." A frown creased her forehead. "...a back-up plan?"

Archer stepped back. "Like what?"

"I don't know. But the tide is turning. We need to get ready." Rayn looked at all of them. She had no more answers. Picking up a splintered piece of wood, she threw it on a pile of rubbish.

Her thoughts roamed. She knew the final response would come at its time, not hers.

CHAPTER FIFTEEN

Seth's voice sounded from the computer room. "They're coming."

No sooner were the words out than the house vibrated, signaling the approaching troops. A silent alarm alerted the farm. The children were hustled to their hiding spot. The house closed up around them.

Dray and Rayn were in the barn talking to Casper, when the alarm sounded. Figuring the barn was safer than the house, they positioned against the wall to be able to watch the drama unfold.

Dray braced himself against the wall, shielding Rayn's back. They watched as Luna, Archer and Galen came out of the house to greet the unwelcome guests.

Bono led the brigade, Milo at his right side. They entered the yard with twenty to twenty-five men behind them. A sunning sight of power and omnipotence.

Pulling up to the small group of three, Bono stopped just short. Balancing his machine between his legs, he removed his helmet, hung it on the handle bars.

His tone full of animosity. "So people, I came to get Dray and Rayn." He smirked at Luna. "I know they are here."

Archer took hold of Luna's hand. "You are wrong General. We haven't seen them for days." He pointed west. "They went off that a way."

Dismounting, Bono strutted up to Luna, disregarding Archer's words. "I think not."

Luna straightened up. "You actually have a thought?"

He back handed her before the other two could react. Suddenly, soldiers were all over them. Two held Archer, two held Galen. The men struggled against their restrainers. Luna kept standing, turning her head slowly back to face her attacker.

Dray felt Rayn's body stiffen. He blocked her from moving by whipping her around to face him. He saw the outrage in her eyes, the muscles in her throat tightened, ready to shout. He silenced her by putting his hand over her mouth.

His eyes bore into hers. "No! You will do more damage than good."

She glared, infuriated at him.

"Trust me." He spoke low, begging her with his eyes.

Looking over her head, he saw Bono grab Luna. Milo came up to stand next to the general. Rayn struggled against her restraints.

"Stop!" He spoke between clenched teeth. He removed his hand, twisting her around to see her daughter taken into custody.

Archer, in a burst of strength, freed himself, lunged toward his wife's captor. Milo hit him with the billy stick he held in his hand. Archer buckled, fell to the ground. Bono kicked him as he handed over a fighting Luna to another solider.

Binding her hands behind her, she was lifted up onto Bono's bike. With one last kick to Archer, he addressed both him and Galen. "Tell Rayn to show herself in twenty-four hours, or..." His last words were full of madness. "...her daughter dies in her place."

He climbed on his bike, took off with Luna hanging on to the back bar to keep from falling.

Galen was released, thrown to the ground. As the dust rose from the departing troop, he crawled to Archer.

As soon as they were out of sight, Dray lightened his grip, allowing Rayn to break away from him, running to Archer and Galen. He followed her. A group of farm people were surrounding the fallen Insurgent. Rayn pushed her way through. Kneeling down by him, she brushed his hair from his face. A large gash on his forehead, blood ran down his face.

Dray stood over them as she placed her hands just above the wound. Closing her eyes, she moved her hands in a clockwise motion.

Archer's eyes fluttered open, the bleeding stopped. His face was an ashen gray.

He grabbed her hand. "Luna?"

Rayn grimaced. "They took her."

Archer closed his eyes, his pain reflected on his face. "No." His words spoken in strained resignation.

Galen pulled himself up to sit next to Rayn. Rayn looked over at him. "Galen, they have my baby."

Galen took her shoulder. "I know." He looked up at Dray. "We'll get her back."

Dray nodded. Already a plan was forming in his mind. But the way Rayn healed Archer's wound reminded him of her healing his wound after removing the chip from his back.

What kind of powers does this woman have?

Rayn stood up as a couple of men helped Archer to his feet. Galen rose next to her. Both faced Dray.

The unspoken question was in their eyes.

What do we need to do?

Dray shoved his hands in his pockets. "We'll get her back. I am already making a plan."

The relief on their faces let him know.

Deliver! Or...

Dray looked over at Archer. He recognized the pain in the young man's eyes. He had felt the same pain when he was told they would kill Rayn.

His mind swirled.

It's time for an all-out assault on the Cartel.

***

Dray paced behind Seth as the young man's fingers flew over the keys. He talked as he worked. "They have taken her to Complex A." He looked back up at Dray.

Dray nodded. "I know where it is."

Seth's voice cracked. "Will they really kill her?"

Dray pursed his lips. "Yes, they will."

"Then we will need to get her out." Seth spoke over to Edward. "Do they still think you are with them?"

Edward nodded. "Yes, I just got a message. 'What are they planning?' What..." He turned to face the two men. "...do you want me to tell them?"

Dray thought for a moment.

What can I say that will make them believe we are being truthful?

"Tell them we are working up a plan...no an attack..."

Seth intruded. "But we are...don't we want to lie to them?"

Dray snickered. "We are, in a way. They think we are incapable of planning a successful attack. Let them get a good laugh over that. Let their guard down."

Edward started typing. Dray watched the words flowed across the screen

They are planning something. It sounds like an attack, but they are ill prepared.

He hit send.

Dray patted him on the shoulder. "Nice touch." He walked over to one of the large screens. "Put up the map of the compound."

Hearing Seth's fingers hit the keys, the layout of the Fort came alive on the wall. As Seth honed in on the compound, Dray saw the set of buildings that made up the complex of prison cells. He pointed to the one on the left that he knew was complex A. Seth enlarged the building's plan.

Dray studied it.

Same place they had held Rayn.

He knew the design well. It was a building connected to the offices. The thinking was that it was the safest. To some degree it was, but it had a flaw. If it blew up the whole military system went with it. The Cartel always felt no one was that crafty. So the logic was to keep the important prisoners close to keep them from escaping. Never did an invasion cross their mind.

Who would dare?

Dray cocked his head, looking at the screen.

Well General Bono, we dare. You taught me well.

Dray tapped the screen. "Print off all you have." He turned as he heard the door slide open. Rayn and Galen entered.

Rayn eyed the large screen. "What is that?"

"That..." Dray winked at her. "...is where your daughter is being kept."

Rayn narrowed her eyes as she walked toward him. "Isn't that the same place I was?"

Dray looked into the sadness in her face. "Yes. And..." He wanted to sound more confident than he was. "...I got you out. I can get her out."

He saw her eyes change from dismay to hope. She looked at him. "You did. What do we need to do?"

Dray looked around her to Galen. "Get your best fighters. We will meet in the dining room in two hours. I know you have enough ammo to blow the compound sky high. I would say now is the time to do it."

He looked down at Rayn. Her face was full of doubt. He took hold of her shoulder. "It's time."

She nodded. This day had been coming for a long time. "What do we do after we destroy them?" Her voice pleading with him to give her an answer. "You know the ones left will come after us."

Dray raised his chin. "And they will find an empty house. We will be gone."

Rayn frowned. "Where can we go that they wouldn't know about?"

The thought hit him like a sledge hammer. "The cabin. No one knows about it. There is a lot of land. And the way they erected the barn, I'd bet houses could be built in just a few days."

Rayn nodded. "Good idea." Her faith returned. She wasn't one to curl up and let defeat overcome her. She would fight. He was glad to see the fight back in her. And the plan...it was coming together.

***

The dining room contained the main players for the Insurgents-Rayn, Dray, Galen, Archer, Seth, Casper and Piper.

Dray unrolled the sheets of paper showing the layout of the Fort. To enter the compound, they would need to come from the south.

Rayn pointed to the outskirts of the Fort. "We have allies over here and..." She pointed to the center of the military compound. "...and here."

Dray looked at her in disbelief.

There had been supporters that close to the compound?

He kept quiet, but thought of how much he missed while his mind was on Rayn. Allowing her to lay out the points of safety, a plan formed in his mind.

When she turned the floor over to him, he knew what to do. "We will strike at twenty-three hundred hours. That gives us enough time to get ready and enough time for them to think we are not ready."

Looking around the group, he saw no opposition.

So far, so good.

"I have a place that we can relocate to. It's safe and unknown, but bare. Housing will have to be built." He looked to Casper and Piper. "Can you get the children and adults ready to go by that time? There is a small cabin there that will provide shelter and the basics, such as cooking and such." He shrugged.

What else would it provide?

Casper and Piper nodded. Casper spoke. "Show us where it's at, we'll get everything ready."

Dray nodded. "We'll leave in an hour by horseback. It's a few hours away. If we travel by night, we'll go undetected."

The couple agreed, turned and left to get things ready to travel. Dray continued. "Galen, Archer get your weapons ready. Everything you got."

The two nodded.

"Seth. Keep an eye on the Cartels movements, but have Angie and Edward start disassembling the computers. You will need to create a new station at the cabin, but keep us connected up to the last possible moment."

Seth nodded.

Standing in front of this group reminded Dray of when he stood in front of his men, giving instructions, barking commands. Only this was different. These people did what they had to do to protect the people they loved. They had a purpose. His soldier's only purpose was to protect a government that made the rules. There was never any connection to the heart.

Dray looked down at Rayn. Her face was turned up to him. She trusted him to make this all right. For her, he would.

Looking again at their faces, he felt a pride. For them and for himself. For once, this felt like a good mission. Never had he felt that before. All his other missions were just routine. No purpose. No reward. This carried its own reward. His daughter would be safe.

Dray dismissed the meeting. Taking Rayn's hand, he pulled her to him. "Sorry I have to leave."

Rayn shook her head. "I understand. I just want you back, soon, safely."

Dray understood her concern. The last man that left her to go help someone, didn't come back. He would.

"Come with me while I get ready."

She nodded, followed him up the stairs. Standing at the door to their bedroom, she watched him drag out the backpack he always had with him. He turned to her with the pack in his hand.

Holding it out to her. "If..." he saw her face frown. "...and I am sure it won't, but if something goes wrong, go through this. Use whatever you need." He removed his revolver from the pack, checked it to make sure it was loaded. Grabbing a handful of shells, he handed the bag to Rayn.

Rayn took it from him, clutched it to her chest. Dray put the gun in his waistband, the bullets in his pocket.

Walking to him, he drew her to him. "It'll be all right."

Her eyes filled with tears, she nodded. His lips captured hers, his arms bringing her closer to him. She melted against him. Kissing her gave him the strength to carry out this part of the mission. He would return to her.

Speaking against her lips. "I will return. I promise." Stepping back, he wiped a tear from her cheek. Letting go of her was hard. She shrank back against the door.

Quickly, he turned away. Bouncing down the stairs, he went to the open bookcase, traveled on down to the nursery. One nurse was in the room. Halo was still the only baby. He walked over to the bassinet. The child looked up as if she expected him. Her violet eyes bore down into his soul.

Slipping both arms under her, lifting her to his heart, he held her close. The sweet smell of a baby wafted up to make an imprint on his heart. Pulling back, he smiled. "I will be back, baby girl. I do this for you, for us."

The nurse came to his side. "I will keep her safe."

Dray nodded. "I know you will."

As the nurse took Halo from him, she whispered. "God speed."

Dray pursed his lips. "He will."

Leaving the two people he loved more than anything was the hardest. Walking through the shelter, he pushed against the trap door that opened in the barn. As he ascended, he saw Casper and several other men waiting beside their horses. Hitting the barn floor with a stomp, he took the reins of Battle Scar from Casper.

Nodding to the others. "Let's go guys. I want to be back here before dawn."

Everyone mounted. Turning the horses around, the posse rode together, Casper and Dray in the lead.

Dray remembered the last time he rode away from the farm. His heart had been broken. Not this time. His heart was eager to return to fight the good fight, to give his daughter and the other children the freedom they deserved.

He kicked his horse and broke into a fast gallop.

Let's get this done.

* * *

Still clutching Dray's backpack, Rayn walked to the end of the hall, on out onto the balcony facing south. She watched as the men on horseback traveled away from the farm.

"Rayn?" Archer spoke behind her.

Rayn's throat was tight, her words unable to come out. She just nodded. She felt Archer's arm surround her shoulders.

Whispering close to Rayn's ears, Archer tried to comfort her. "He'll be back."

Rayn wanted to scream.

Can you guarantee that? Tell me so I know!

Archer kept trying to talk. "It won't turn out like Heath."

How do you know?

But she kept her negative thoughts to herself. She needed to believe he would return. Her shoulders shook as the painful memories returned again. She had buried them so deep. Now they were real again. And so were her fears.

* * *

Looking at Heath's beaten and lifeless body, Rayn refused to allow the god-awful pain to consume her. Reaching out she touched the cool skin on his arm. Her spirit was hurting, her soul dead.

"Did he suffer?" She asked back over her shoulder to Galen.

She heard his silent attempt to answer. Jane was beside her. Wanting to touch her, comfort her, but Rayn shrugged her off.

"Galen, tell me." She spoke low, trying to not let her emotions overtake her.

Clearing his throat, Galen spoke in broken words. "Yes...they beat him...I could hear his screams...it seemed to go on forever."

Rayn tore her gaze from Heath to face Galen.

Galen couldn't look at her. His eyes were downcast. "I'm sorry, Rayn. It happened so fast..."

Rayn placed her hand on his shoulder.

163

Galen raised his eyes to hers. "I am so sorry."

Rayn bit her lower lip, nodded. Turning to face the people standing around. "We need to cremate him immediately." She sighed. "I don't want Luna to see him like this."

She looked at Casper. "Prepare the site." With one last look at her husband, Rayn walked away to tell her young daughter her father was dead.

As the two stood before the flaming scaffold that held the body of Heath clad in pure white linen, Rayn vowed to never love again. It was too painful.

Harding her heart, she watched her husband turn to ashes.

Done.

But her heart was at a loss as to what to do next. That was when she found the Rock.

***

Coming back to the present, she leaned her head against Archer's. She knew she would have to deal with whatever came.

Weighing her situation.

Luna was being held a prisoner.

Dray was gone.

They had been given twenty-four hours. They needed more time.

Pulling away from Archer, she patted his cheek. Slinging the back pack over her shoulder, she strutted down the hallway. Turning, she look backed, saw Archer standing frozen in the same spot.

She barked at him. "Let's go. We need to buy more time for Luna."

Throwing the bag in her bedroom as she passed, it slide across the wooden floor. Hustling down the stairs, she went to the computer room.

Seth was sitting, watching the screen as the horsemen disappeared from view. The sound of Rayn's entrance made him turn.

Rayn placed her hands on his shoulders. "Tell me what's happening."

"Well...actually the Cartel took the bait. Well, the general did. I think Milo is smarter than him."

Rayn tightened her grip. "We have more time?"

"I think so. The last message was more in celebration of an attack." He looked up at her. "I think they are welcoming it."

Rayn patted him. "Good. Let them believe we are incapable of such a thing!" She looked around. Edward was working on the bank of computers against the wall. She walked over to him.

He turned at the sound of her approaching footsteps. She locked eyes with him. "Have you found your people?"

He nodded. "I finally got in touch with my sister. She is aware of our contacts, but she has to lay low. But..." His face beamed. "I know where they are kept at night."

Rayn nodded. "You make plans to get to them when we attack. Get them out of there."

"But...but...I am no fighter." Edward stammered.

Rayn smiled. "Then learn quickly how to be one. This will be your only chance to save them."

The realization on his face said it all.

Rayn shrugged. "It's now never."

He nodded. "I understand."

She turned away. Her spirit was in sync with her obligations. She lifted her shoulders high, winked at Archer who had followed her into the room.

"It's time to rock and roll."

CHAPTER SIXTEEN

The group of riders flew across the wide-open plains. The late afternoon sun kept the day at a prefect temperature.

Casper pulled his horse up to a stop. Dray followed suit, but didn't understand what was going on. Battle Scar turned in circles.

The rest of the men also stopped their steeds. Dray finally got his horse to stand still. Looking around, his eyes fell on the large rock. "Damn." He said under his breath.

He heard Casper's low chuckle. "Been here before?"

Dray nodded his head. "Hell yeah. Whipped my ass the last time, sent me back to the farm.

Casper raised an eyebrow. "I take it you tried to debate with the Power."

Dray looked over at him. "You could say that." He looked up at the sky. It was a clear blue, not a cloud in sight. No wind, no lightening, no thunder. "It's quiet today."

Casper nodded. "It's giving us its blessing."

"I take it you've been here before." Dray eyed him.

Casper smiled. "We all have." He looked back to the other men. They nodded in agreement.

Dray shook his head. "Figures." He kicked the side of his horse. "Let's go. I want to get there before dark." Secretly, he was relieved that the Power had allow them to pass without incident.

Turning now to the west, the rest of the ride was uneventful. Dray was relieved when they came over the crest and he saw the cabin below. The sun was just setting over the lake. The colors of evening, pinks and oranges, welcomed the weary travelers.

Dray led them down to the cabin. Dismounting, he tied Battle Scar to a post, walked into the place he had loved since a child. Now it felt like a haven, a protection from the storm.

Casper followed him in. "Wow, this is great."

Dray looked around the small space. His eyes settled on the bed, where he first made love to Rayn. His gut told him to get back to her. "It's all yours. Do what you need to do." He turned back to the door.

Casper grabbed his arm. "You heading back?"

Dray nodded. "I want to get back. Take care of things here?"

Casper released him. "Will do. God speed."

That's the second time someone has said that to me.

He nodded. Walking out, he found his horse being watered and fed. Stopping to look around his place, he was filled with a satisfaction that this would be the new home for the Insurgents. And his daughter.

The overwhelming desire to return to her overcame him. As soon as Battle Scar snorted to signal he was ready to ride, Dray swung up into the saddle.

The man patted the horse's hindquarters. "God speed."

Dray looked down at him, a frown creased his brow. Taking one last look around, he nodded, turned toward the east.

Darkness was falling quickly. Allowing Battle Scar to travel at a good, but easy pace, Dray was glad to be on the way back. He knew Rayn was worried about him returning. He wanted to be back with her, finish this battle and move on.

Suddenly, Battle Scar stopped. Catching Dray by surprise, he soon realized where he was again.

The Rock!

Speaking to the clear night sky, he addressed the many stars above him. "I know you are here. If you have something to say, spit it out. I want to get back to Rayn and Halo."

The quiet that surrounded him make him uncomfortable.

Surely there is some epic commandment I need to know before going into battle.

Still quiet.

"Fine. I'm leaving."

Battle Scar didn't move. The horse stood still, silent, ignoring his rider's commands.

"Seriously?" He nudged his horse again.

Nothing.

He addressed the night sky again. "Spit it out, ole' great one. I need to get going."

He was not as brave as his words implied. He ducked a little as he spoke the words.

Before his eyes, a vision appeared. Silas and Helena stood together, holding hands, smiling at him.

His shoulders slumped from the grief he finally felt at losing them. "This isn't fair."

They want you to know they are with you.

"I knew you were there."

I am always here.

Dray chuckled. "Yeah, I know." He focused on the images before him. He could feel the love radiating from them. To their right the lone figure of a man appeared.

Dray sucked in his breath.

Heath?

The transparent figure nodded.

Okay, this is weird. Meeting the ghost of my lover's dead husband.

Not weird. It's to give you the blessings of the ones that went before.

"Even Heath?" Dray found this very strange.

Especially Heath. You are protecting the love of his life and his daughter and...

Dray narrowed his eyes. "...and?"

His grandchild.

Dray was taken back. "Luna is pregnant?"

It would seem so. Your mission is to get her out of the prison and safely to the new camp.

Dray frowned. "Does she know?"

Not yet. But she will figure it out soon. Time is of the essence.

Dray understood...well not everything. He looked at Heath. "I do love her."

Heath nodded. "I know. I wanted that for her. To have someone to stand with her, to have her back."

With those words, everything made sense. Dray watched as the vision faded. "Good-bye mom and dad. I know now how much you loved me. I am sorry I didn't see it before." A sadness engulfed him.

Their words were carried by the soft breeze. "We know. We understand. Our love will guide you. Go forth in confidence."

Dray looked across at Heath. The two men nodded at each other. Understanding passed between them. Then the vision was gone.

Dray sat for a moment. Battle Scar snorted, pawed the ground.

You know your quest. Go! Do what you do best.

Dray raised the reins, saluted the sky, turned toward the north.

At a breakneck speed, Battle Scar carried Dray back to the farm. Dray leaned low over the saddle. He wanted to be back with the two women he loved. He couldn't get there fast enough.

***

Rayn tried to keep herself busy to keep from worrying about Dray. Working with Piper, they planned the evacuation of the farm. It was hard to leave the place she had created. But it had become unsafe. Plus, her daughter's life was at stake. Rayn would move heaven and earth to save her child. After all, this is what it was all about.

Piper had placed everyone in groups. They would move one group at a time, so hopefully the exodus would not be tracked. The first group would be ready when Casper returned.

At about midnight the two women went to their beds. Confident that they had taken everything they could into account.

170

Rayn, work weary, walked into the empty bedroom. Her heart was so heavy. Her first thoughts were of her daughter. Going to the window, she gazed out into the dark night.

Stay strong, baby. We will get to you.

She bowed her head, praying to the One who had always protected her.

Please make this all go right.

The voice crashed over her, giving her the strength she needed. **All is set. You have a hard battle ahead of you. Fight strong, trust the people I have sent to you. And trust me.**

Rayn's thoughts went to Dray. Her love for him was different than her love for Heath. She had met Heath in easier times, had fallen in love with a common future. Heath was her equal. They shared the same thoughts, shared the same heart. And though their love they created Luna. She could still feel his spirit around her.

But the love she had for Dray was unique. They started as enemies. She fought hard against the attraction she felt for him. Accepting it was only physical, since she had been without a man for a while, she figured it was just her hormones.

She chuckled to herself.

Damn urges.

But he had proved to be more than a lover. His destiny was to free them. Her soulmate, her spiritual fighter. Wrapping her arms around her chest, she feared for him.

I trust you, and him. Just give me a sign we are going the right way.

The midnight sky lit up with a shooting star streaking across the darkness. Rayn felt the peace, the promise of victory and protection.

Thank you. I am grateful for all you have provided.

The wind from the open window circled around her.

All is well. Rest. Dray is on his way back. He has just reached the Rock.

Rayn threw her head back and laughed.

You know he hates that.

The voice's tone held a chuckle as well.

I know.

Rayn left the window, lay down on the bed for a quick nap. Her weariness quickly sent her into a deep sleep.

That was until her eyes flew open and she knew Dray was home.

***

The early morning dawn crested as Dray rode down the final embankment to the farm. He had never seen such a welcome site.

Home was a strange word to use. No, not so strange, he was back with the ones he loves.

Greeted at the barn by one of the workers, he slid off the sweat-soaked saddle. Patting Battle Scar's hindquarters, he spoke to the man taking the reins. "He has been ridden hard. Take good care of him. He deserve it."

Shaking his shirt, Dray started walking in the direction of the house. "So have I."

Suddenly he saw a figure running toward him.

Rayn

In an instant she was in his arms, her legs wrapped around his waist. Burying her face in his neck, he felt her body shake.

"Darling..." her body felt so good. "...It's all right."

He felt her head nod against his neck.

Allowing the moment to last, he relished the feel of her body in his arms.

Feeling her legs release from his waist and slid down to the ground, he held her away from him. Frowning at her tear-stained face, he kissed her tears, the salty taste exploding on his tongue.

Rayn took his mouth in hers. The kiss was strong and passionate. He returned the same to her. His latest experience at the Rock freed him to love her as he meant to do, as he needed.

Lingering in their embrace, she pulled away first. "I am so glad you are here."

172

Dray wiped her still damp cheek with his thumb. "So am I."

Walking arm in arm, they went to the house. Rayn leaned on his shoulder. "How was everything?"

"Fine. Casper should be here soon."

"The people are getting ready to leave."

He squeezed her into his side. "Good. Now we need to get to concentrate on our plan to attack the Fort." He felt her shudder. "Are you okay?"

Rayn nodded. "It's just so surreal. I knew this day would come."

Dray stopped, turned her toward him, holding her by the shoulders. "We will be okay. We can handle this fight."

Rayn looked deeply in his eyes. "I know. I just want my baby safe."

Dray grinned. "Speaking of babies. How is Halo?"

Rayn smiled at him. "She is fine. She's in the first group out."

While it stabbed at his heart to send her away, he knew it was for her safety. Taking a deep breath, he raised his head to look over hers. "She will be safe. She has angels watching over."

Rayn pulled his head back down to look him in the eyes. "Angels, huh? You've come a long way, Lieutenant Konner."

CHAPTER SEVENTEEN

After a shower, holding a hot cup of coffee, Dray stood in the kitchen watching the first group of people get ready to leave. He felt a presence at his elbow, turned and saw the nurse holding Halo.

His baby girl's dark purple eyes were wide open, a small crooked smile played at her tiny mouth. He sat down his cup, scooped her into his arms.

Leaning close, he kissed her little button nose. "Stay safe, honey. I am right behind you." His voice cracked as he finished. "I love you." The words, while odd to him, sounded so right.

Reluctantly he handed his daughter back to the nurse. He trusted the woman, as he trusted everyone here. He had made sure that she knew to take the baby to his cabin. From what he gathered from Casper, work had begun on the new houses.

Yes, houses.

Several of them to accommodate all the many families that had fled from the Cartel to seek sanctuary at the farm. Where they got the lumber was still a mystery to him, but it was not going to keep him up at night. They did what they needed to do.

Watching the nurse walk out the door, his eyes followed them through the windows as wagons and carts appeared. Picking up his cup, he walked out to the deck. Standing at the railing, he studied the first group to leave, comprised mainly of women and children led by Casper.

Casper had returned mid-morning. He had given the directions to the cabin. The other groups would leave every hour. Casper was leading the first group back.

Footsteps sounded behind him. He felt Galen before he saw him.

Galen placed his hands on the railing. "It's really happening."

Dray took a big sip, then a deep breath. "Yeah, it is..." He let his news spill forward. "...I met Heath."

A small smirk played at Galen's lips. "How was that?"

Dray chuckled. "Weird."

"I bet."

Dray turned, looked at Galen's profile. The unfazed look on his face was not a surprise. Galen turned toward Dray, leaning one side on the railing. "So, what did you two talk about?"

Dray gave him a wry smile. "He told me he was okay with me and Rayn."

Galen shrugged. "I figured that."

Dray frowned at Galen. "Why didn't you connect with Rayn? You two are so close."

Galen looked down at the floor. "Rayn is my sister."

The news took Dray back. "I didn't know that."

"Most don't. It's just something we have kept to ourselves."

Dray looked back over the yard, the convoy was departing. "That explains a lot."

"How so?"

"You always believed in me, never thought of me as a rival."

Galen copied Dray's line of vision. "I knew the first time you rode in here on your crotch-rocket, you were sent for her."

Dray knew the knowledge and the acceptance was real. "You could have told me."

"Would you have believed me?"

"No."

"Well, there you have it."

Dray shook his head.

What the hell!

***

Dray, Rayn, Archer and Galen joined Seth and Edward in the secret command room. Angie was sent ahead with some of the equipment to start the new computer system.

A large print-out of the Fort lay before them. Each building, each road, each alley had been tagged.

Dray pointed to the military buildings. "The offices are in this building on the north end." He moved his finger down. "Luna is in this part of the building." He felt Rayn bristle next to him. He had not revealed to her the message he had received at the Rock of Luna being pregnant. He was afraid it would alter her strength to rescue her daughter.

Archer stood, observing Dray's instruction.

"We go through the southeast gate." Dray looked around the group. "I can get us to her cell..." He pointed to one small square. "...we will exit through the east door. It is closest to the east gate...Can we get our bikes there?"

Galen nodded. "We will have them there for you."

Dray turned his focus to Galen and Archer. "How many fighters do we have?"

Galen spoke. "Many."

Dray had not expected such a vague answer. "Seriously? How many is many?"

"Thousands. Half of them are inside the Fort. They will grant us access."

Dray was speechless.

Rayn stood over the printout. "Where are the children?"

Dray had not expected this question. He pointed to a building above the military offices. "Why?"

"We need to get out as many as we can."

"And do what with them?"

"Take them to the new compound. Some have parents there. Some of the parents are in the Fort. They all have waited far too long to get to their children."

Dray was still surprised at their reach, the resources they had so close to him. "How did the ones in the Fort get away with not being found out?"

"They were sleepers. They fed us information, helped us with supplies..."

The lumber!

Dray chuckled to himself.

If Bono had known it was taken from his own Fort, that the lumber was used to build his enemy's houses, he would have a fit.

"...they will be ready to fight as soon as we get there. They will get as many children as they can out before everything blows sky high." Rayn turned to Edward. "Your people?"

Edward smiled. "They are in contact with the ones inside. They are ready..." He looked over at Rayn. "...thanks for helping me get them to safety. Especially after what I did..."

Rayn held up her hand. "You did it from the heart. That makes a difference. I would have done the same thing."

Dray could feel the bond between all of them, him included. And it all felt right.

"Okay..." Dray clapped his hands together. "...we roll at midnight."

All five fisted their hands in the center of the table over the print out of the Fort that was soon to be no more.

CHAPTER EIGHTEEN

The night quickly brought the needed darkness for the Insurgents to gather for the fight. Dray grabbed Rayn's as she paced in the large room. The look in her eyes told him of the anger and pure hatred she was feeling. A spark of fear danced in her jaw as she glared at him.

He knew he was not the source of her anger, but he felt the fire in her. "We'll get her back." He wanted his words to calm her, but they seemed to have the opposite effect.

"I'll kill him if he has harmed her. . ." Her words were spat out.

Dray knew better than to disagree with her. "If we need to we will." He felt her arm relax, but just as quickly it tighten up again. She was not going to let her guard down, not even to him.

The Insurgents came forward to group. They carried military guns stolen by the group in the Fort. Dray couldn't help being impressed. When he had planned the raids on the farm, he had no idea they were so heavily armed. They could have made minced meat of him and his troops. The fact that they didn't made the realization of how focused they were on just doing what promoted their cause without doing any more harm than necessary.

The friction was almost like a bubble that surround the group. Dray had only witnessed this much comradely in the service. To see a group of Insurgents form such a task force was a phenomenon he had not expected. The Cartel had well underestimated the band of men and women that would fight for the right to raise their own children. His thoughts went to Halo.

Yes, he would fight as hard as they to preserve her right to know him as her father. His life had come full circle, he had left one side, joined another now he stood in the night to waited for his chance to fight the enemy.

Rayn took Dray's arm, together they stood before the crowd. The people were talking quietly, waiting for the next direction.

The group quieted as Archer stepped out on the deck above them. Behind him stood Seth, Edward and Galen. Looking for guidance, they waited for him to speak. His voice cracked and that only brought more determination to Dray to get Luna back. Not just for Rayn, but Archer too. A foreign feeling came over him, causing him to stare down at Rayn.

What if I lost her? I could tonight, this is serious.

And he knew that better than anyone else. People die in battle and tonight would be a massive battle. The Fort group and all the outlying farms were coming together from all sides. They were going to take down the Cartel tonight.

"You all know the plan." Archer shouted into the night.

With his hand on her back, Dray felt Rayn's body stiffen. Having her daughter capture made her powers surrounded her like an aurora, but her rage engulfed her spirit. Her eyes told him that until this was over, Rayn would be powerful with a white hot fury.

Dray sighed at the thought of Bono sleeping quietly in his bed, unaware that tonight would be the demise of the world as he knew it.

The band of people from the farm walked or rode horses. Men and women dressed in black warrior garb walked steady and sure over the rough ground. They avoided the road, too easy to see them coming.

Rayn walked off by herself, Dray walked beside her. It would take about an hour to get to the town. Approaching the outskirts, silently, people walking and on horseback joined them. The crowd grew larger until it was supporting a thousand or more. Rayn showed no sign of fatigue or hesitation. Dray had marched into battle before, but this was Rayn's first time in combat. Only her bitterness kept her from being afraid. Understanding her feelings, he let her walk slightly ahead of him, slightly apart. Her back was straight, her arms held her weapon at chest level.

Dray's motorcycle would be waiting for them as soon as they got Luna out. Galen had moved the cycles to the town one by one. Coming to the top of the hill, the band of people stopped. Surrounding the Fort on all sides were thousands of people. The darkness of the night covered them like an invisible shield. Under the radar, the sentries at the computers would not see them coming. Their clothing covered their body heat.

Dray had not known the small group on the farm had gathered so many followers. For once, he was glad he was on this side of the fight. Not just because it was so massive in numbers, but he felt he was fighting for the right Cause. This was not going to be a win or lose fight. The Cartel had underestimated the Insurgents when they took one of their own. They would get her back and there would be hell to pay for it.

Galen came up beside Dray. "This is it. One group of Insurgents will march right into the Fort, hopefully it will create a diversion. We will go to the prison, hope that all of Seth's program's work and get Luna out, then haul ass out of here. There will be a lot of fighting, but just keep on going. The survivors will join you at the lake."

Dray's head snapped around to look at Rayn.

The survivors.

The cool, unemotional way he said it ran a chill down Dray's spine. Rayn's cold, steely eyes told him that was the way it was. He remembered the icy eyes that lied to him, told him there were no children when he would raid the farm.

Archer came to the small group, passing through the crowd. They slipped down the hill and crouching low, headed straight for the south gate. The muffled sounds of marching feet echoed across the valley. Shouts could be heard from the Fort.

It was on.

The west side of the compound burst with explosive fireworks, leaving the east side open, unprotected.

Rayn would not allow Dray to help her. She moved like a lioness ready to protect her cub. He followed, didn't want to be too far from her. The Cause was only her second priorities, her daughter was her first. She had kept all of this going for Luna. If they did not get Luna out, she would die before she gave up. This he knew. This he had accepted. This he would not let happen.

Their bodies hit the brick building, softly and quietly, Dray took the lead. He had the key card to open the doors. Slipping it soundlessly into the slot, he watched as the light turned green, pulled the door open. With no sound, the other three followed. Their steps were silent as they moved down the cement hallway to the next door. Again, the green light blinked and they were in the section that held Luna's cell. Luna had on a tracking devise that Seth had slipped to her through their allies in the Fort. They knew which cell she was in.

Passing each cell without incident, the other inmates were looking out the windows at the fight, their backs to the intruders. Reaching cell number five, Luna stood at the bar doors. Her face was thin and drawn, but the light in her eyes showed how grateful she was to see her rescuers.

Dray again slid the card in the door, with a soft click Luna pushed the door open from her side. Into the arms of Archer she flew, her face streaked with tears. But, being her mother's child she quickly took the extra weapon from Galen, nodded she was ready to go.

Silently, they moved back up the steel-railed hallway to the second door, slipping through one barrier at a time. As soon as all but Dray were on the other side, he slipped the card across the master lock to the cells. With a loud grating sound all the cell doors opened. The shouts and screams from the prisoners covered any sounds that the Insurgents would make. Safe on the other side, as the prisoners were still locked in the cell room.

With Dray leading, they took a turn left when they had come from the right. Dray knew his way out of the faculty, and was specific about where they would emerge. Their means of escape should be waiting for them. Pushing the door open, Dray stuck his head out, convinced they were alone, he motioned the rest to follow. As per instructions, his motorcycle and two others were waiting. Holding the door to make sure no one followed them, Archer and Luna climbed on one motorcycle. Galen on the other. Rayn stood next to Dray's, her helmet on ready to jump on behind him. His boots crunched softly on the gravel.

"You really are one of them." The voice of General Bono shattered the quiet. All turned to look towards the five soldiers that stood, guns drawn, waiting for the command.

Dray straightened, turned to face his arch enemy. He could feel Rayn move up behind him. He wished she had just gotten on the cycle and ridden away.

"You doubted me." Dray was buying time. He wanted the attention to stay on him and away from the others.

General Bono strolled in a relaxed, cocky way toward his former officer. "Not doubted, just thought you would chicken out. Return to the only way of life you knew. Military."

"Galen." Dray shouted over his shoulder without taking his eyes off the general, "Get them out of here."

The roar of starting motorcycles was his answer. He could now feel Rayn's hand on his back. "Rayn, go." His voice was calm, his command clear.

She didn't answer but he knew she hadn't left.

General Bono's sarcastic laugh echoed against the buildings. "She doesn't obey you as well as your men did.

"Check. It was a standoff. "Rayn." His voice pleaded. "Go with them."

Still no answer, but he could hear her take a deep breath as she readied for a fight. The sound of the two motorcycles leaving faded in the distance.

"Stop them." Bono commanded the soldiers. Four of them left, one stayed behind the general. Dray nodded to Milo.

"Now I have my prizes." The pride in his voice was unmistakable. General Bono turned slightly to the other soldier. "See, I have the warrior woman and the deserter. I can show the people what will happen if they cross us.

Rayn slipped her hand into Dray's. He squeezed it. If they were going to die they would die together. Both still held their guns.

Dray wanted to end it now. Go out in a blaze, maybe take one of them with him. But if he took that course, Rayn could also die. He wasn't willing to make that choice for her. It only took a spilt second for Bono to lose his focus. So intent on his accomplishments he forgot whom he was facing.

His gun only lowered a fraction, but it was enough for Dray to raise his unnoticed, fire at the hated man. The bullets from Rayn's gun flew at the general the same time as Dray's. Milo was knocked flat on his back by Bono's heavily falling body. It was the only thing that kept the bullets from hitting him.

Dray and Rayn turned in unison, jumped on the cycle together. Dodging the patrols who were trying, with no luck, to corral the intruders, they wove through the calamity in the streets. In a split second, they were down the alley, out of the Fort; headed the same direction Dray had taken Rayn when he had freed her. Her arms were wrapped around him so tight it hurt his ribs. But it was a welcome pain, for it meant she was alive, she was with him and Bono was dead. Motorcycles kept joining them as they flew over the rough terrain of the countryside. They were on their way to a new home. The war wasn't over, just stalled long enough for them to regroup.

CHAPTER TWENTY

Dray sat on his deck, holding Halo, his precious gift of life. The rest of the Insurgents had reached the lake just before dawn. Three houses had been erected since the pilgrims relocated to their new home.

Several new families had joined the group. They were the loyal Insurgents who had been living in the Fort. New children arrived, some the sons and daughters of the sleepers, but some freed with no families. They would have to adjust to freedom and be reprogramed to stand up for the right to stay free.

Halo moved in his arms, snuggling down into her daddy's chest. He now knew what all these people fought for, why they stayed loyal to a once small, but now mighty band of people willing to risk everything to keep the children safe.

The people moved about the new homes. Animals sounded the call to a new day. How long peace would be granted was unknown, but for now it was enjoyed.

Dray kissed the top of his daughter's head. He felt the quietness of the Universe surround him.

All is well.

"You know they are going to come after us?" Rayn's voice sounded from the doorway.

Dray looked over at her, how he wished they could just live a simple life, but he knew that would not be in their lifetime.

"I know."

***

General Milo led the pack of soldiers up to the familiar farm house. Only, the house was burnt to the ground, no sign of life anywhere. No people, no animals.

The attack on the Fort had been brutal, well-planned and executed. The number of people now missing was phenomenal. He had no idea he had been surrounded by so many of the enemy.

His Fort lay in shambles, his leader dead, a handful of loyal soldiers remained. He took the rank of general, as he was the last remaining officer standing. Word had come from the Cartel headquarters to regroup and find those **damned** Insurgents.

Milo had to chuckle, damned they were not. They must have had help from a higher power to pull off their coup.

Milo swung one leg over the cycle, planted both feet on the ground. He hung his helmet on the handle bars. Walking up to the charred ruins, he kicked a half-burnt board.

Where did they go? Couldn't be far. They left quickly. It would take months to rebuild.

He looked around. There were many secrets hidden here and he meant to find them.

Where to start?

Milo wiped the sweat from his forehead. This was like a huge jigsaw puzzle with a million pieces.

Let's get started.

Milo walked into what was left of the house, shouting over his shoulder to his men. "Search the barn. We are looking for something to tell us where they went."

Made in the USA
Coppell, TX
27 August 2022